"Chekov Plot"
by
Andrew Johnston

ISBN 1 872350 91 7

Copyright 1996
Andrew Johnston

**Published by
"Criffel Books"
Anwoth
Dumfries
Scotland DG1 4AX**

Chapter 1

Just south of Glasgow Green lies a tract of derelict wasteland, known as "The Blazes". For some who are old enough this name is still evocative of images of the factories and foundries that used to characterise the area, the lights and flames of which would light up the night sky like majestic beacons and symbols of industrial pride. They had all closed a long time ago and were either demolished as they became deemed to be a hazard to passing traffic or were simply left to fall apart themselves. In their places lie squares of land neatly marked out by redundant streets; empty except for piles of refuse and rubble. Most of the tenement buildings that housed the population of the area have also been knocked down or have had the entrances to their common closes barred with large "condemned" signs. Only two or three still stand. The flats within them have all been subjected to a stream of constant vandalism from drunk itinerants, gangs of roaming youths or transient squatters. The remaining few residents of the area have all witnessed the decline and learned to contend with the ravage as part of their daily lives.

Like an oasis in this desert stands a public house, "The Derry Bar". The flats that used to sit above it have been demolished and the pub alone occupies the site of the main cross-road. For the four decades up to the late 1950's when the neighbourhood was at its industrial zenith, the bar used to serve the army of workmen that tended the furnaces and workbenches, with welcome refreshment. At the close of shifts it would quickly fill up with all varieties of tradesmen and labourers anxious to wash out of their mouths the taste of the dirt and dust that they had gathered during their day's toil.

The pub had been bought a few years after the last war by an Irishman, James Sullivan, who immediately changed its name to reflect his home town and emphasise the new ownership. Sullivan had come to Glasgow a good number of years previously as a labourer. He always knew that he would not return to Ireland and started to look around for a means of providing a livelihood for his family. He managed to save a modest sum of money from his work but he received a windfall after he learned in a letter from his brother that his father had died and the rest of the family had decided that they no longer wished to remain in farming.

The farm was duly sold and Sullivan received his share of the capital realised. That same day he visited his future bank manager and one of the large breweries in the city. He knew that they were anxious to establish a number of tied houses where they could be sure of an outlet for their product. Before he returned home Sullivan owned a public house and had completed his application to the city's Licensing

Board.

For many years, ''the Derry Bar'' provided a good standard of living for the Sullivan family. When he became of age the oldest son, Peter, started working in the bar. It was always understood that he would inherit the business. The other children were encouraged to pursue their educations as far as possible for they would have to take their chances in the vagaries of the job market, but Peter's future seemed secure. This notion, though, was called more and more into question as the area went into decline. It soon became painfully obvious that the future of all the small businesses were inextricably bound up with the prosperity of the heavy industries. As factory gates closed for the last time so did more and more shops in the locality board up their windows and seek either to conduct their business elsewhere or simply cease to exist.

One particularly quiet night after the last customer had left Sullivan was counting the day's takings as his son swept the floor. Suddenly the older man slammed the till drawer shut with a force that caused his son to stop and enquire what was wrong. Sullivan looked at his son for a moment and then said,

''We're not going to be able to carry on for much longer on the strength of takings like tonight.''

''Every place has bad days, dad. Tomorrow will be better.''

His father stared at him in exasperation before

continuing through gritted teeth.

"No it bloody won't Peter. There's just not enough folk around anymore. Old Sloan found that out last week when his wee dairy shop had to close down. Two years ago he was doing a roaring trade selling filled rolls at dinner time. Now where's he going to get a job at his age? We'll go down the same plug hole unless we do something about it. Are you just going to wait for that to happen or are you going to do something about it?"

Peter realised that this was not just another moaning session from his father but an invitation to talk about developing a business survival strategy.

"What about selling up and moving into the city?"

"No, that wouldn't work son. Nobody's going to buy in this area until it has been redeveloped and that could be years away. Too late for us anyway"

"Maybe I should start looking for a job."

The publican looked at his son, suppressed the cruel laugh in his throat and shook his head, "As what? You've got no qualifications. I had a shot at being a labourer and I don't want you following those footsteps. I've worked too bloody hard for the wheel just to turn full circle."

Peter had by now put away the broom and was leaning on the counter looking at his father. The lights at the front of the bar had all been turned off as he had completed cleaning these areas and the only source of illumination was now the lamps that shone around the publican as he stood by the till. Even on this stage Peter did not see the expression of despair that he had expected.

"So you got any ideas, Dad?"

"Just the one. It's been with me for many a year. Almost an old friend now. Thought of it first when I was a navvy. You get plenty time in that job to get lost in your thoughts. And, in fact, the first thing I did when I took over here was to put a little bit of it into practice - but there's more to be milked out of this sacred cow. I'm sure of it."

Sullivan poured himself a large whisky, before he elaborated.

"The punters can get booze anywhere and if that's all we can sell them then they'll find shops nearer their homes. But we can give them something else and keep them drinking here"

Peter was confounded and lost.

"What else can we sell? All we know about is the licensed trade."

Sullivan was smiling now. He moved round the bar and came right across to his son.

"We can sell them Irishness."

"Sell them what?", asked the son incredulously.

"Irishness, Peter", continued Sullivan. "Listen to me carefully now. A number of customers have told me that one of the reasons they come in here is because it reminds them of home. Now I'm sure that half them wouldn't even know which direction Ireland is but that doesn't matter a toss. If changing a pub's name gives folk a comfortable feeling that makes them spend money on drink, think what we could do if we tried.''

Peter joined his father in a smile. He knew of pubs up by the University where at certain times people queued to be allowed to enter. He wondered whether it would be possible to emulate that popularity and was at the age where all new ideas are automatically and inevitably linked to a conviction of success. He jokingly asked his father whether he thought that it would matter that he had never set foot in that island.

Sullivan's smile broadened into a laugh.

''Not at all, son. We're talking about myths and illusions. The reality as far as I can remember it wouldn't be attractive to anybody. I couldn't get out soon enough.''

''Well there are certainly plenty of people in here that take every opportunity around to tell me about their Irish granny. How would we actually go about it though? What would you do to make the pub more 'Irish'?''

Sullivan despaired at the lack of imagination and business acumen in his son. He replied curtly. ''Peter, there are times when I give up on your ability to run this business. Any fool can stick a shillelagh up on the wall or stick a few leprechauns behind the bar. But think about it, think hard about it... You can do better than that.''

It was noticeable that the ''you'' in the sentence had been emphasised.

''You mean 'us', Don't you dad?''

''No, Peter I've done enough. I decided a few weeks ago that I'm going to retire. I just wanted to give you a little bit of hope with the shop and this is the best I can do. We're at a new start here; it's up to yourself to see it through. The idea is my present to you. I'll help but I'll not interfere. I had to make it myself. The only advice that I was given when I set out to come across the water was to work out every decision by looking at whether or not it was going to put a shilling in my pocket. I did that when I bought the pub, I did it when I was offered jobs. You use it too to work out how far you want to take the idea.''

Even as his father spoke ideas were crystallising in Peter's mind. He had married Isabel the previous year and she was constantly accusing him of living and working in his father's shadow. Now, he thought he had been presented with the opportunity of showing his wife and father just how capable he was.

The following Sunday, father and son set about repainting the walls green with an orange and white border to replicate the Irish flag. Peter wrote off to Borde Failte in Dublin and secured a number of posters reflecting life in rural Ireland, which were duly tacked on to the newly painted walls.

It also seemed to be commensurate with this new strategy that stronger links were forged with an already recogniseable Glaswegian symbol of Irish heritage, Celtic Football Club. When one of the customers suggested the formation of a supporters' club for that particular football team, Peter followed his father's advice. He reckoned that he might lose some customers but it would be likely that he would gain more. He secured various autographed photographs of current players. These were then prominently and proudly displayed above the gantry. The pub was actually fairly conveniently located for Celtic's ground. A short walk across the Green and through Bridgeton would take the supporters to Parkhead, but it was sufficiently far removed from the main thoroughfares to provide easy parking for cars. It also provided a convenient pick-up point for the coaches to take supporters to visit the grounds of other football teams. This was quickly recognised and every Saturday of the football season the bar heaved to a tide of green and white scarves worn by an army that was more than happy to spend money on drink.

But the ''Derry Bar'' came to be ubiquitously recognised within the city as more than a pub for particular football supporters. It was busy at most other times with customers whose families had been part of a great diaspora but who had not managed or wished to travel very far from their homeland either in geographical or emotional terms. Here they could pretend that they shared a common heritage with all the other customers that at once bound them as an elite extended family and at the same time set them apart from the other cultures that prevailed in Glasgow. New customers seemed to arrive daily almost as though the exodus was still taking place and the émigrés were congregating in the "Derry Bar" like some Ellis Island. New customers brought new names and new stories to the pub. Peter was pleased with the way things were working out and played his part. He ensured that all the staff he was required to employ to satisfy demand had at least Irish names and if their arrival was sufficiently recent to allow them to retain an Irish accent then so much the better. Copies of the previous day's "Irish Times" and "Irish Independent" were left at a corner of the bar for customers to read. Guinness stout and Jameson's and Bushmills whiskey became the most popular orders.

The clientele also dictated ways in which Sullivan's now vindicated strategy would continue to be implemented. One evening just a few weeks after Peter had taken over, a man extricated himself from a small company of people, came across to the bar and gestured to Peter in a way that indicated that he wished not only to order drink but also to speak to the landlord on a matter of protocol.

"Do you see that man over there?"

Peter nodded as a gentleman in the centre of the company was pointed out to him.

"Well, that's the brother-in-law and he's just here on a wee holiday from Birr." Peter had no idea where this was but was sure that a more relevant point would soon be made and allowed the man to continue. "Now it so happens that he's one of the best singers in the whole of County Offaly and we were just wondering if yourself would have any objections to him giving us a little tune."

"You're sure he can keep a note in his head? I get enough caterwauling from drunks."

"On my mother's grave, Mister Sullivan. You'll be fair impressed."

And indeed Peter was impressed, as was the rest of the pub who fell silent to listen to the traveller's renditions of various Irish classics like "The Mountains of Mourne", "Molly Malone" and "Danny Boy". It didn't completely escape Peter's notice, however, that the loudest applause was for the nationalist anthem "A Nation Once Again".

A number of regulars approached Peter that night to say how much they had enjoyed the singing and hoped that it would be repeated in the near future. Once again Peter considered his decision in terms of whether it might increase business. There was found to be no shortage of singers, albeit of varying quality, willing to stand up. They recalled in song, romantic images, heroic deeds, tales of unrequited love or cruel injustices from the actual and mythical past of the island that was generally described as "The Old Country" in this particular bar. The nights of Irish singing gradually became more formal. A microphone and speakers were installed and a master of ceremonies employed. Peter at first considered taking over the M.C. role himself. He quickly realised, though, that the job required not only skills in persuading sometimes diffident talents to come forth but also to be able to fill in with a few songs when there was a temporary lull in the proceedings. Consequently Arthur Reilley who had been one of the most enthusiastic of volunteers to stand in front of the microphone and whose loquaciousness, humour and bonhomie was generally acknowledged, found himself in part-time employment in the very place where he was now spending a good portion of his leisure hours.

Sullivan lived for only eighteen months after he announced his retirement, but by the time of his death not only was the "Derry Bar" the only remaining business in The Blazes but it was renowned in the local licensed trade as being one of the most profitable pubs in the city.

Peter took several days absence shortly after

his father's funeral to play golf in Perthshire. When he returned he let it be known that he had in fact been to the native heath in order that he could disperse his father's remains over Lough Foyle. Those who saw the widowed Mrs Sullivan scatter ashes in the Garden of Remembrance at Linn Park Crematorium just a few miles from the pub must have wondered. They did not raise the matter though, as it seemed totally appropriate that the custodian of this sanctuary of Irish culture should make that special pilgrimage to the birthplace of his ancestors.

One evening in the late 1960's a very attractive young woman with long black hair walked across the pub to take the microphone. Reilley saw his employer watching her but mistook the source of his admiration. He sidled up to Peter and whispered, "This'll be good. That's Tom Barry's grand daughter. She'll be singing about her granddad. I've heard her before in here"

The whole audience held a complete silence for the duration of the song. It seemed to Peter that he was the only person there who didn't know who Tom Barry was or understood the esoteric significance of the song. He listened to the lyrics for clues.

"On the 28th day of November,
    outside the town of Macroom
The tans in their big Crossley tender, were
    hurtling away to their doom."

As in most pubs it was customary for staff to

have a drink together, after closing time and once the place had been cleared for the following day's business. That evening, Peter made a point of inviting Reilley to join him at one of the corner tables.

"So, are you going to tell me what the song was about and besides being that young lady's grandfather, who was Tom Barry?"

Reilley jolted his head back and looked at his employer.

"Are you kidding me, man? Do you really not know your own country's history."

"Not that bit. Are you going to enlighten me or not?"

Reilley was more than pleased to give a history lesson.

"After the '16 Easter uprising failed, the struggle for a united Ireland went on. The Brits used the Black and Tans to torture civilians and burn houses in their attempt to destroy the IRA. But we were more than a match for these bastards. In 1920 just before we got London to concede the Free State, Tom Barry stood in the middle of the road to make a constabulary patrol stop. The bastards threw away their rifles when they realised they'd been ambushed, but when Barry's boys went to accept their surrender they pulled pistols out and started to fire. Barry kept his head though and ordered them all to be shot down."

Peter was taken aback by the use of the pronoun "we", but did not feel inclined to enquire any more deeply into Reilley's political allegiances. Instead he sought confirmation of his understanding of the song's significance.

"So this Tom Barry was a member of the IRA.?"

"Aye, of course. One of the first. He had been a soldier in the British Army and was made a commander when he joined the volunteers."

"And most of the punters knew that story before the girl sang?"

Reilley was surprised at the level of ignorance being demonstrated by the question.

"Sure, you've got a lot of good Republicans amongst your regulars. Did you not know that?"

"Well I knew that the rest of the city sees this as a Celtic pub maybe even as a Catholic pub, but I've always welcomed anyone who keeps a civil tongue in his head and doesn't look for credit."

He had, however, learned an important lesson and the opportunity to use it followed fairly soon afterwards.

In August 1969, R.U.C. reservists with submachine guns and tear gas grenades chased rioters through the streets of Londonderry. When the rioters fled into the Rossville Street flats a huge Irish tricolour was unfurled. This event was caught by both television and newspaper cameras and broadcast throughout the world. It became the main topic of conversation in the ''Derry Bar'' and it was only a matter of time till someone sought Peter's view on the matter.

''I think it's a fucking disgrace that Irishmen can be chased by armed thugs through the streets of their own country. Jack Lynch should send guns up from the South, then we'd teach the B Specials what its like to be chased.''

Nobody could recall Peter speaking with such passion before and all agreed that he had a great deal of insight into both the problem and the solution.

A week later John Dillon came into the pub for the first time. He was a small man in his early thirties dressed in a conservative blue suit under a waxed green Barbour jacket. He ordered an orange juice from the barman and asked if he could speak to the owner. Peter looked at him before going across and assumed that he must be a sales rep., although it was unusual to get such callers in the early evening.

''Hello there, I'm Peter Sullivan, the owner. I hear you want to talk to me.''

The small man, who spoke with a Belfast accent, introduced himself by name and assured Peter that he would not beat about the bush.

''I heard about your little speech the other night and some of my friends and I were mightily impressed with your ideas.''

This did not sound like a sales pitch and Peter was temporarily confused. ''What speech are you talking about?"

"The one about arming the folk in the Bogside."

Peter's confusion turned quickly to irritation. The articulation of his views had not been meant for public consumption.

"What the fuck has that got to do with you?"

"Calm down Mr Sullivan. We're on the same side. I just wondered if you would like the opportunity of assisting the efforts of some people who are prepared to take the matter further?"

"What do you mean 'assist'?"

"Do I have to spell it out Mr Sullivan? The real Republican Army is the one that wants the six counties returned and is prepared to fight and die for them. But we need your help to buy the tools for the job. I'm not asking you for money. I just want your OK. to organise regular collections amongst your customers."

In retrospect Peter thought that he should have anticipated such an approach being made in a blatantly obvious Irish pub but it took him completely by surprise. At first he didn't know how to respond; then again he remembered his father's advice. He wondered about that shilling in his pocket. He knew that people did not have an infinite amount of money to spend and if they were being asked to put some of it in a collection box then it might drive them elsewhere or at the very least mean that they would have less to spend on drink in the "Derry Bar". He thought about offering a contribution from his own pocket but realised that it would have to be anonymous and that would be of little benefit to him.

"I'm sorry, Mr Dillon, I can't help you. It's a house rule that I'm the only man that collects money around here and I do that by selling drink."

He expected some sort of an argument from Dillon and had already decided that he would just have one of the barmen throw him out. He was surprised then when Dillon simply thanked him for his patience in listening and expressed the hope that this approach would not preclude him from visiting the pub again.

"Not at all Mr Dillon as long as you don't bother me or my customers you and your money are very welcome here."

Dillon became a regular visitor to the bar. He would call in a couple of times each week but unlike other customers he studiously avoided engaging in the communal banter. He was always well dressed with a collar and tie and although the suit was occasionally changed for a sports jacket, he was never without the Barbour jacket which remained worn for the duration of his stay. The routine of each of his visits was exactly the same. He would order a soft drink from the bar, if Peter was around he would give a brief nod of recognition, find an empty table and unfold a copy of the Glasgow Herald. He never instigated conversation with anyone. If he was addressed he would respond politely but succinctly and in a manner that conveyed he had no wish to continue discussion. When he finished his drink he would fold up his newspaper and carry his empty glass over to the bar, give a pleasant smile of thanks and depart.

He was unlike other customers in another way. They either tended to belong either to the football supporters fraternity and come in only on a Saturday or be regulars who preferred to frequent the pub at other times. Very few customers crossed this divide, but Dillon was one whose self imposed isolation afforded him the same level of comfort and ease in either crowd.

Several months after his first visit, he was sitting at one of the window tables which he favoured. It was a Saturday lunch time but Celtic were playing in Edinburgh that day and the supporters had left in their coaches an hour or so previously. Consequently the bar was unusually quiet. Peter knew the half dozen customers that remained. He could now enjoy less busy spells confident in the knowledge that the hordes would return and had even allowed one of the two barmen to leave an hour before the end of his shift.

The whole pub turned around to see what was happening when they heard the swing doors thrust open with such a force that caused both of them to batter off the walls. They saw eight young men all in their early twenties spill into the bar. Each of the newcomers was wearing a blue, red and white scarf indicating his allegiance to Rangers Football Club whose perceived anti-Catholic employment policy and links with other Protestant symbols made it an anathema to the customers of the ''Derry Bar''.

When they reached the counter one of them barked at the remaining barman.

''Gie us eight pints of lager.''

The barman looked to Peter who was now standing at the other side of the bar exchanging pleasantries with two of the few customers that remained.

''That's OK, Sean'', he responded. He also suggested to the customers with whom he had been talking that they might like to leave in case there was to be any trouble. He quickly and surreptitiously explained that if the Rangers supporters had no-one with whom they could start a quarrel it was more likely that they would leave peacefully.

The other regulars saw Peter's friends leaving and heard the deprecatory remarks about the Celtic players, represented in the photographs behind the bar, grow louder and louder. They, then, also decided that in this instance at least, discretion may be the better part of valour and chose to depart. Dillon alone who continued to read his newspaper, apparently oblivious to the developing altercation, remained. Sitting silently in a secluded corner, he was hardly noticeable.

When the beer had been drawn and the glasses set on the bar, the price was communicated to the one who had placed the order.

"Whit? Ye want money? I heard that if you gave a wee song in this pub they give you a free drink. I'll give you "The Sash". That'll be worth a few pints, eh?"

The barman tried to smile as he replied, "Sorry pal the singing's no till the night. It's strictly cash only the now."

One of the group picked up a glass and took a large gulp of his beer. He then promptly spat it out, spraying it over the barman.

"Call that lager. It's mair like nuns' piss. We're no paying for that. Gie us some whiskies."

The rest of the gang then picked up a glass and tried to empty the contents over Sean. Peter brought them to a halt when he shouted.

"OK, stop it - now! If you don't like the beer then just go. There'll be no charge for it as long as you don't come back."

Another of the strangers spoke this time. "Who the fuck are you? Are you trying to bar us?"

Peter answered both questions. "I'm the boss in here and aye, the lot of you are barred – for good."

Peter heard the head butt crack against the bridge of his nose before he fell to the floor. He recognised the warm trickling liquid passing over his lips as blood. And then he heard the shout. "That's it Ronnie, teach the Feinian bastard a lesson". But Ronnie needed little encouragement. As soon as Peter was on the floor he had started to kick him. Peter curled up into the foetal position and then put his arms around his head in an attempt to protect himself. His assailant screamed at him.

"Don't try to tell me where I canae go. This is my country and if you don't like it you can fuck off back to the bogs."

It seemed that that was a signal for the rest of the gang to throw their glasses at the gantry. Sean ducked to avoid the splintering glass. Peter rolled over a few times until he reached a table then used it to pull himself up. As soon as he no longer felt the sting of the kicks, he shouted, "Sean, phone the police."

Sean tentatively moved towards the telephone but before he could reach it another of them had vaulted the bar, grabbed him by the hair and pushed a large bread knife up to his face.

"Chib the bastard," ordered Ronnie. The man with the knife was smiling at Sean's imprecations, but saw Dillon rise from his seat and start towards the bar. Dillon had his Barbour jacket unbuttoned and was holding it open with his left hand. His right hand was deep inside the poacher-pocket. Ronnie stepped forward to block his path.

"You canae go to the wee boys' room just now

Napoleon. You'll have tae haud it in."

Dillon smiled at the allusion to the position of his arm.

"Oh, very good my friend. Here's another one. What's the difference between an apple and an orange?"

One of Ronnie's colleagues responded this time.

"Your fucking mental pal; I hope they sort that out in the hospital as well." Dillon continued to stare at the man blocking his path and answered the riddle himself.

"You can't get an apple bastard."

The man holding Sean behind the bar laughed and said, "Hey Ronnie that guy just called you an orange bastard. Dae something about it, will you?"

Ronnie drew a flick knife out of his pocket and pressed the button at the end of the handle. A stiletto blade sprang up. Almost simultaneously Dillon whipped his right arm out of the jacket pocket. When it was fully extended it pointed directly at Ronnie's head. At its end Dillon's fist tightly gripped a pistol. There seemed to be the sound of a collective intake of breath. But it was left to Dillon to speak in a harsher Belfast accent than Peter had heard him use before.

"Yir man has told me that this here Webley and Koch point two two is pretty limited both in terms of range and accuracy. But since we're having such an intimate and cosy chat I don't think there's really that much doubt that it could sever your brainless skull from that bag of lard that doubles as your body. Do you?''

Not a sound came from either the very ashen faced Ronnie or from any of his colleagues. Dillon went closer, put his free hand around Ronnie's neck, pushed the barrel of the gun into the soft flesh of the cheek and screamed. ''I'm talking to you, you bastard. Fucking answer me!"

"O.K. Keep the heid wee man. We're going. We're going now. No problem, all right." whispered Ronnie. Dillon poked the gun again into the cheek.

''Bloody right you are, too.'' He made a sweeping action with the pistol. ''All of you bastards, piss off out of here.''

The one behind the bar climbed across to join the rest as they cautiously retreated. When they got to the door they broke into a run and collided with one another in their simultaneous efforts to get out. One braver soul though could not resist a last futile act of defiance. He stuck his head round the door and before pulling it away again very quickly, shouted at no-one in particular ''fuck the Pope''.

Dillon ignored this and instructed Sean to climb above the opaque part of the window to see if they had a motor car.

''They're all scrambling into a big Commer van.''

"Get the registration number".

Sean repeated the number. Dillon carefully wrote it down, held it up to allow Peter to see and then put the note in his wallet.

Chapter 2

Peter was holding a dish towel up to his face to staunch the flow of the still streaming blood, but he managed to say with noticeable enthusiasm.

"That was bloody brilliant Dillon. Bloody, bloody brilliant. I owe you one. Is there anything I can do the now?"

"Yeah, you and Sean can keep quiet about the gun. My bosses would be pretty pissed off if they thought I was courting publicity with the firm's tools."

Peter understood but he looked at Sean for some acknowledgement of the request.

"Aye, no problem wee man. I did'nae see a thing."

"Good, keep it that way", responded Dillon. "The other thing you can do is get me a large whisky. My knees are shaking. I've never had to pull a gun out before."

It was near enough the official closing time for Peter to lock the doors. He told Sean to take the evening off, that he would find cover and then muttered something about having to arrange some security. Dillon offered Peter a lift home suggesting that he really was not in a fit state to drive.

As the key of the large padlock on the outside door was being turned, Peter noticed that parked right behind his car was a newly registered VW Golf. These were the only two cars in the vicinity. If one of them was left until the pub re-opened there was a high risk that even if the vehicle itself wasn't stolen then removable parts like tyres and the battery would disappear. Peter considered this for a moment but concluded that Dillon was correct in his assessment of his ability to drive. He told Dillon that he stayed in Burnside and that if he started to drive east towards Cambuslang he would give him more specific directions in due course. They arrived at the Sullivan's house in a little over twenty minutes. It was a sandstone house sitting at the end of its own drive and surrounded by a well tended garden; the kind of building described by estate agents as a "detached villa". The house and the neighbourhood were very tangible symbols, though, to Peter's success in business. When Dillon remarked more out of courtesy than interest that it was a nice home, he learned how proud Peter felt about the house and what it indicated about him.

"Not bad at all, is it, considering when I first got married all I could afford was a single end in a tenement building in the Cathcart Road? Do you know my father worked all his life and was over fifty before he could afford to leave his flat to buy a house like this?"

He stopped and laughed at the small joke that he was about to tell himself.

"One where the stairs are on the inside." He looked at Dillon for an appreciation of his humour and the grimaced smile was disappointing.

"You had better come in, John. Have a cup of coffee and it will give me a chance to show you around the house. At the very least I need you to help me explain to Isabel what happened today and why I'm in this state."

Dillon mused on the use of the two Christian names. He was mildly impressed that Peter remembered his, but noted that it had taken him until now to start using it. He guessed that Isabel could only be the Mrs. Sullivan with whom his prospective host had shared that single end in Cathcart Road. He hoped that the proposed trip around the house might slip Peter's mind once they were actually inside. He already knew the function of this proposition and wasn't interested in any confirmation of the Sullivans' social status.

He momentarily recalled the occasion when he had been invited for a briefing session in a distinctly middle-class estate of neat, brick houses in the little seaside town of Bangor. Commander Charles McLean was just about to bring the assembly to some form of order when the host had asked if anyone would care to look around the rest of his new prized possession. The invitation was peremptorily declined by the Commander telling him in tones that unmistakeably conveyed his irritation, not to be so bloody stupid. McLean had previously spoken of his disdain of middle class pretentiousness. Pride withered to a stump of embarrassment for their host, as the Commander emphasised this point by continuing to berate through ridicule.

"The only houses that are interesting enough to look around are those for which you pay an admission fee or those that you are considering purchasing."

As Dillon was instinctively locking the car, he noticed that Peter's return was being observed from an upstairs window of the next house. Neither man, however, could guess the significance that this observation post would play in the drama that was to unravel and enmesh their lives several years later.

Isabel opened the door to them and an expression of surprise came over her face when she saw the blood stains covering her husband's clothes.

"Oh my God! What's happened to you? Are you alright?"

She was also looking at Dillon and wondering about his part in whatever had occurred, but felt that answers to the questions, already raised, would be enough for the moment.

"I'm OK, lets go inside", said Peter jerking his thumb in the general direction of the watching neighbours.

Isabel stepped aside to let the two men pass. Peter conducted the introduction as he walked by her.

"This is a customer of mine, John Dillon. He

was a big help sorting out a bit of bother we had today.''

Isabel was still concerned about her husband's well being and could not be persuaded to leave the hall until she had been satisfied that the bleeding from his nose had stopped. Her husband also managed to convince her that while it was still painful to touch it did not feel as though it was broken and hence would not require any medical attention at this juncture.

The party eventually managed to negotiate its way into the main public room. They all sat down and Peter recounted the events in the pub that afternoon.

Dillon felt that the description of Peter's courage, particularly when he informed the gang that they were barred and exhorted them to leave, was slightly exaggerated. Aghast registered on his face however when the detail of the gun was mentioned. Peter failed to pick this up and continued as though to emphasise the point.

''Oh, you should have seen that bastard's face when John pushed it into his face. I swear that he peed himself. And then they fell over themselves trying to get out the door.''

Isabel asked what seemed an obvious question to her.

''So have you let the police know?''

Peter was imbued with a feeling of bravado through telling the story and expressed this in his response.

"What would the police be able to do? We sorted it out ourselves; they got a right fright. They won't be back. Believe you me. Go on make us a cup of coffee, love."

Isabel understood why Peter's father had occasionally expressed despair of his son but she chose not to deride him in front of a stranger. Instead she excused herself. She also suggested that Peter should wash and change his blood stained clothes.

She left immediately after this suggestion to find clean towels for her husband. This provided Dillon with an opportunity to halt his host's intended departure by grabbing Peter's jacket sleeve and roughly pulling him down again into his seat.

"What did you tell her about the gun for? I thought we agreed we would keep that bit to ourselves."

"Aye, but you didn't mind me letting Isabel know surely? She's my wife. She won't breath a word of it. I'll make sure I tell her that it's to go absolutely no further. Don't worry."

Dillon did look worried. His voice became quieter and Peter had to strain to hear his admonition.

"Look, Peter it's not a game I'm mixed up in. It's serious stuff. If word got out about what happened today the probability is that the police would come round asking questions about the gun. And if my friends thought you were speaking to the police I couldn't guarantee your safety." A changed expression now covered Peter's face.

"Are you threatening me, Dillon."

"Not at all Peter. Don't go getting hold of the wrong end of the stick. I'm just telling you about the need for secrecy in my line of work and also that some of the characters we ask to enforce it are, well let's say that they wouldn't be the most savoury of house guests."

Peter came uncomfortably to recognise that Dillon was telling him that his own safety might be in jeopardy should he inadvertently mention the gun. The idea of being given such a direct ultimatum in his own house, though, was not one to which he took kindly.

"OK. But I'm a big boy too, now. I can take care of myself."

"Of course you can, Peter but if I can help you then so much the better. Look take a note of my phone number, just in case you need to contact me."

Dillon wrote a telephone number down on a scrap piece of paper and handed it to his host. As he was doing so Isabel returned. She was accompanied by a small black poodle who ran to sniff at Dillon. It was obvious that he was not at ease with the animal and Isabel went across to pick it up. She introduced the dog to Dillon as she was doing so.

"This is our child substitute, Toto."

"Isabel!", rebuked Peter.

"Are you still here", she rather superfluously enquired of her husband and then continued to explain the reason for her interruption.

"Does Mr Dillon want something to eat with his coffee?"

Peter started to answer vicariously in the affirmative, but Dillon contradicted him to explain that he had a dinner appointment later and indeed would have to leave shortly.

"With your wife Mr Dillon?"

"I'm a widower Mrs Sullivan. It's a business appointment."

Isabel felt that Dillon was giving her the impression in the tone of his voice that further enquiries would not be welcomed. She turned to her husband.

"What's that piece of paper?"

"It's John's phone number. Put it on the table will you and I'll copy it into the book later?"

Peter then managed to excuse himself, this time without hinderance and followed his wife out of the room. Isabel returned by herself a few minutes later with a tray holding three cups of coffee. She kneeled to put it down on a low table beside Dillon and as she did so he studied her intently. He gauged that she was a few years younger than her husband who, he felt, was a contemporary of himself. That meant, he calculated, that she would be in her late twenties. She was a tall woman; taller in fact than either Dillon or her husband and would be euphemistically described as being well made. In the language of a previous generation she might have been referred to as a "handsome woman". She had long red hair and Dillon guessed that like her husband she may also be of Irish descent. She was wearing a pink V neck sweater that was both loose fitting and cut low. This allowed Dillon to notice the black lace bra strap that came over her shoulder. He smelled a strong pleasant perfume that emphasised her feminal qualities. It occurred to him that this fragrance had not been present on the previous occasions that she had been in the room and he wondered whether it may have been applied for his benefit. As she leaned over the table Dillon's eyes followed the gradually revealing bra strap until he could see the extent of the fullness of her breasts.

When he was younger, Dillon had lived with his mother at his grandparent's house. His Aunt Kathleen also stayed at home then and although she was only six years older than the young John, she appeared to belong to a completely different generation. She epitomised glamour, sophistication and excitement as he passed through puberty and sexual awakenings.

The size of the house and the number of inhabitants left little room for the preservation of modesty. He watched Kathleen wash at the jaw box sink in the kitchen and when she returned to apply her make-up in front of the large mirror that hung above the mantlepiece, he was still there. She became aware of the furtive glances being cast in her direction and would smile at him. This was not only motivated by her feelings of familial warmth, but she was also flattered by his attentions and would tantalise him by such ploys as holding her dress up just a little longer than was necessary to fix her suspenders.

He could not fully understand the stirrings that Aunt Kathleen precipitated in his developing body. They floated constantly around his mind and the scent of seduction emanated from them. He was content though to sink deep within these feelings and let them wash over his incipient manhood.

His grandmother had caught him on more than one occasion masturbating as he lay in bed thinking of Kathleen. She had chided him and told him that self-abuse was a sin. He would surely dispatch his mortal soul to eternal damnation should he engage in that practice ever again. This threat could not diminish his clandestine desires; rather it enhanced the sensation of excitement. This moment with Mrs. Sullivan became redolent of these pubescent awakenings.

Isabel noticed the silence and could also feel the lascivious gaze on her. She looked up and caught Dillon's stare. He immediately became embarrassed and started to blush but she held her smile as she asked. "How do you like it, Mr Dillon?"

"I'm sorry, Mrs Sullivan", came a stuttering response.

"How do you like your coffee? Do you take milk and sugar?"

"Just milk. Thanks."

Isabel could not help but notice the nervous strains that had crept into his voice and was mildly amused by them. When they had settled with their coffees she said to him.

"You haven't taken off your coat. Is that because you want to hold on to your gun?"

"Not at all Mrs Sullivan. The pistol was only an imitation you know and I think I left it in the car anyway."

"That's a pity. I don't think I've ever had anybody in my house with a gun before."

"As I said, Mrs Sullivan, it's only an imitation."

She ignored this claim and continued. "Some women would find the idea of a man carrying a gun very sexually exciting."

"Oh, I think I'm past the stage of exciting anybody at all, in any way."

Again she continued as though oblivious to his contribution to their discussion. "What could be more phallic than the idea of a long barrel that shoots bullets!" She looked up to observe his reaction and noticed that the red glow on the skin of his face was still present. Again his embarrassment caused him to stutter. "Peter's not down, yet. Perhaps he's decided to have a bath. Anyway I have to be going myself. Tell him, will you, that I'll pop into the pub again soon."

She showed him to the door and thanked him for bringing her husband home. As Dillon walked towards his car he was very conscious that she had his phone number. That evening Peter held court in the pub. The bruise on his nose, the damage to the gantry and the return of those customers who had prematurely departed all signalled that there was a story to be told. As the only eye witness to the events that was now present, Peter took on the role with relish, again lingering a little bit longer on his part. He did, however, ensure that he failed to recount the specific reason why his attackers chose to follow Dillon's exhortations to leave at that precise moment and any questions in this area were fielded with imaginative, humorous or simply vague answers.

Chapter 3

A few weeks after his visit to the Sullivan's, Dillon's sleep was abruptly interrupted by a telephone call.

"John, It's Peter Sullivan here. Any chance you could come over to the house."

"Sure. Tomorrow morning OK?"

"No. I was hoping that you might come tonight."

"Peter, it's three in the morning according to the clock beside my bed. Did you hear that 'beside my bed' I'm in my kip. Now it's not that I don't appreciate the invitation but can't it wait till a time that normal human beings are up and about?"

Peter was obviously in no mood to appreciate humour. He continued with a note of urgency in his voice.

"I know the time, John. Honestly if it wasn't important I wouldn't have bothered you at this hour. Can I send a taxi round for you?"

"No, it's alright. The car's outside. If you're telling me it's that crucial that I come just now, I'll be with you in half an hour."

"It is, it is."

The car made a crunching noise as it came up the gravel path which was clearly audible in the silence that characterises the hour before postmen and milkmen take to the streets. The door was opened as Dillon approached it and Peter ushered him into the public room that was used on his last visit. Isabel sat in one of the armchairs but made no effort to greet him. He was invited to take the other armchair. Peter offered him a drink and when it was declined went across and sat on the empty settee before speaking.

"John, we've got problems. A couple of nights after that incident in the pub I got half a brick through the window. I thought if that's their revenge then I'd just leave it at that. But another week later somebody threw a lemonade bottle with petrol in it into the doorway of the pub. Luckily somebody who was just coming in for a drink saw it happen and shouted on us."

"Did you manage to put the fire out?", Dillon queried.

"Yes, we were lucky I've got one of those fire blankets and I got that on top of the flames and just shuffled around on it while some other guys threw buckets and basins of water on my feet. Bloody best pair of shoes ruined."

Isabel viewed this last piece of information as an unnecessary digression and suggested in reprimanding tones that he proceed.

"Then today something happened which has really upset Isabel." Peter hesitated for a moment, then continued, "And me as well. Toto, the dog, was killed. Isabel found him lying at the front door gasping for breath. There was a bit of meat besides him that someone must have shoved through the letter box. Isabel put him in the car and rushed him to the vet. He was spewing up all the way there but died just as she reached the surgery. I doubt whether the vet would have been able to do anything for him anyway. They have arranged to do an autopsy on Toto, but I'm sure they will just find out that he's been poisoned.''

Peter stopped at this juncture but Dillon neither said anything nor changed the expression on his face. Peter felt uncomfortable in the silence and continued, ''John I'm scared. Bricks through the window of the shop is one thing; even trying to set fire to the place I could have coped with. I'd just arranged for a few blokes to act as bouncers and we would have taken care of anybody who tried to bother us in that way again. But attacking my home, that's different altogether. Christ!, Isobel was in herself when the meat was stuck through the letter box. What would have they done to her if she had gone to the door when they were there. What sort of folk are we dealing with? Who would poison a wee dog?''

There was no-one willing to answer the questions. Peter looked at Dillon before he explained the exact reason for his request for this immediate visit.

''John, Isabel and I have been talking. We feel that we don't really have a choice now We've got to involve the police. I'll have to tell them about that

Saturday afternoon, but I promise I'll not mention either your name or the gun.''

Dillon looked in a very deliberate fashion at Peter then Isabel; then returned his gaze to Peter. On this occasion he responded, ''I'm glad you asked me to come over and have a chat before you did anything.'' He stopped and waited to see whether there would be any contradictions forthcoming, then decided to check his understanding in a more positive way.

''You haven't contacted the police yet, have you?'' Peter shook his head before he elaborated on this reply.

''No, no I wanted you to know about it before we went ahead, but Isabel's keen that we do something before anything else happens to us.''

''I understand. But I have to tell you that it is my experience that the police are not that terribly good in dealing with this sort of thing. I think they believe that if you are mixed up in that sort of activity you probably deserve what you get. Guilt and innocence become unnecessary concepts.''

For the first time Isabel spoke to him. ''So what do you suggest? That we just take it until the bastards get fed up dishing it out.''

Peter was surprised at the acrimony in her voice but it was explained as she continued. ''Peter has told me who you're with, Mr Dillon and I'm not scared. I'm a Catholic and like a lot of us over here

I think you've got a point. You were sold short when Collins signed the Treaty that kept the six counties out and the only way you're going to get them back is to fight for them.''

Both her husband and Dillon were surprised at her knowledge of Irish history and would have told her so had she stopped long enough for them to intervene. She continued her tirade, however, with anger becoming more and more recognisable.

''But I'm not going to let my sympathies get in the way of me protecting myself. Peter can do what the hell he likes but I'm going to the police. I'm sorry if that steps on your toes Mr Dillon but I can't help that.''

''You are a very determined lady, Mrs Sullivan. I'm sorry about the wee dog and I know that you must do what you think is best. The reason I'm suggesting you don't go to the police though is not really about stepping on my toes. You've told me now about your intentions so I can take the necessary precautions. Even if you hadn't, my people have got inside sources of information amongst the peelers and one of them would probably have let me know. If the police find out about the gun all that will happen is that I'll be pulled out of Glasgow. I might have my wrist slapped for making an error of judgement in trusting Peter, but the worst they can do is that my next posting is more likely to be Newry or Lisburn rather than New York or London. It's not the most heinous of offences." He let a moment of silence heighten the impact of his next statement. "I couldn't promise you though that you wouldn't get a wee reprimand from my people as well."

This was the second time that Peter felt the sense of a threat being made in his own home by Dillon. He decided from his previous experience not to pursue it but rather to pick up the cue to ask the question that Dillon was inviting.

"So what do you think we should do?"

"I thought that there might be some recriminations from that day. I just had no idea that it would go any further than stone throwing, but that's why I made a point of taking down the car registration number and as I said we've got some guys in the police force who help us out with information. I've already found out that the van's registered to a guy called Ronald McAteer."

The name reminded Peter of his ordeal. "Hey, the guy that nutted me was called 'Ronnie' by his pals."

Dillon peremptorily dealt with this observation before continuing, "It might or it might not be the same guy. 'Ronnie' is not that an uncommon name. The point is if this McAteer was one of them then I'll recognise him. If he wasn't then I'm sure he will know who he loaned his van to that day. I've also checked that it hasn't been reported as stolen. One of the things we are good at is persuading people and

I'll take along one or two experts in that field."

"What if you don't manage to 'persuade' them as you call it." Isobel's sarcastic tone made it quite clear that she still preferred her strategy.

"Don't worry Mrs Sullivan. I can guarantee that you will not be bothered again once my friends have a wee chat with whoever is responsible for this."

"Where does this McAteer stay?" asked Peter, more sympathetically to the idea.

"A place called Larkhall. Do you know where that is?"

Peter laughed, "I might have known. The Orange Free State." He saw the quizzical look on Dillon's face and explained.

"Not the one in South Africa. Larkhall's in Lanarkshire. It's a Protestant ghetto. All the Billy's are shoved either there or Airdrie when they get a council house and the Tims are put to Coatbridge or Holytown. Handy for the Carfin Grotto, I suppose."

Isobel was surprised when Dillon indicated that he didn't know what the Carfin Grotto was, but explained it to herself by the notion that even if he was a Catholic he wasn't a West of Scotland Catholic. Dillon continued to talk about his solution and convinced Peter that it would be worth trying. He in turn tried to persuade Isobel. "Come on Isobel. What have we got to lose? There's no way it will be tied back to us. Isn't that right, John?''

Dillon assured them that no matter what happened they would not be implicated. He also addressed Isabel's anxieties by noting that if the recriminations were going to increase in severity they would probably do so for as long as the ''Derry Bar'' remained open. He concluded his point by noting that if the attacks continued he would voluntarily quit the country which would give them leave to contact the police without fear of reprisals from his side.

By the time they had agreed that the Sullivans would allow Dillon an opportunity to resolve the issue in the manner he had suggested it was almost dawn. They all rose at the same time to signify the end of their discussion. Dillon was watching Isabel as she stepped out of the chair. He again felt a sexual interest awakening in him and had to make conscious efforts to suppress it. He noticed that she was wearing no make up and was dressed in very casual clothes. Her movements alone, however, as she walked in front of him across the room precipitated both immediate excitement and desire.

She held the outside door open and as Dillon crossed the threshold she said to him. ''The start of something new, eh Mr Dillon?'' Dillon blushed again. He was conscious of Peter standing directly behind.

''Pardon.''

''Dawn. The start of a new day I hope it will

be better than the last one.'' Dillon nodded at Isabel's explanation He moved his head to catch Peter's attention.

"I'll pop into the pub in a few days to let you know how I've got on."

"I'm going to stay at home for the next week or so. The staff can run the bar themselves. But now those bastards know where I stay, I want to be here in case they try anything on with Isabel"

"I understand. Best of luck."

Chapter 4

The Volkswagen drove around the streets of the council housing estate. The buildings, colloquially but unimaginatively described as "four in a block" were essentially large cubes with a slate roof. Two doors at the front gave access to the downstairs flats. Around each side, concrete stairs led to the doorways of the upstairs flats. The houses had been built by the Local Authority no more than two decades ago, but already the area was recognised throughout the County as an undesirable place to live. Many of the windows were broken and remained un-repaired. Others had wooden hoardings over them, indicating that the dwelling was uninhabited and it occurred to Dillon as he surveyed the area, probably uninhabitable. He also noted that there was a large number of children playing in the streets, which surprised him in view of the fact that they had just seen others enter the local primary school to start their day.

The gardens had at one time been protected by small and pleasantly coloured fences Most of this fencing was now broken and those parts that still stood either had their paint peeling off or were held together by obviously rotten wood. The gardens themselves without exception had been neglected by their custodians. Even though it was winter, Dillon could see that their most important function, in recent times at least, was allowing dogs to relieve themselves.

The car turned into McAteer's street. Dillon's two passengers whom he simply addressed by their surnames, Egan and Smith, studied the numbers of the houses. ''There it is, on the left'', noted Egan. Dillon slowed as he passed the address but continued around the corner before stopping. After he had parked the car he went round and unlocked the boot. Inside it was meticulously clean and empty except for a tool box and a bulging white plastic bag. He took the plastic bag and the three of them retraced the last part of the car's route. The address that interested them was one of the ground floor flats with its door facing on to the street. His two companions positioned themselves with their backs to the wall so that they would be out of the line of the direct observation of the small unkempt woman with a child's arms around her waist. When she opened the door, she neither smiled nor spoke but maintained a vacuous expression on her face as she intently examined the stranger at her door

''Is Mr McAteer in?'', enquired Dillon when he realised that the woman was only going to continue staring at him.

Before he received a reply, a man came out of one the rooms that adjoined the hall, naked from the waist up and with bare feet.

He shouted. ''Whit dae ye want? Are ye fom

the Social?"

"No McAteer, I'm not from the Social. There's another wee business that's outstanding."

As soon as he recognised the Belfast accent McAteer, turned and ran through the door with the dirty paintwork, flaking with age, at the far end of the hall. Mrs McAteer tried to shut the front door but Dillon pushed it back on her with such vigour that it caused her to bounce off the wall. The child started to cry. Dillon waved his two companions into the house. They pursued their prey through the opening at the far end of the hall and into the kitchen. McAteer already had a window open and was scrambling over the sink to escape, when he felt four hands grab and pull him back. He was thrown roughly across the kitchen and afforded the opportunity to face his attackers. The woman had followed the party and now stood in the doorway shouting at them. Undeterred, Dillon deposited the bag that he had been still carrying and roughly pushed her out of the room. As he was closing the door he warned that if she tried to interfere then not only would she suffer but so too would any children that they found in or around the house. She instinctively knew that he would have no compunction or hesitation in implementing this threat and discretely withdrew. Meanwhile, McAteer saw both Smith and Egan pull a short wooden truncheon, the sort normally carried by policemen, from inside their jackets. They started to hit him around the head and shoulders. McAteer tried with limited success to fend them off by guarding his head with his bare arms. After a dozen or so blows had been delivered the torrent stopped, more suddenly than it began. McAteer retained his defensive pose for a few moments longer, then tentatively dropped his hands to see what was happening. He regretted this decision almost immediately. As soon as his face was cleared he saw Smith deliver a back hand stroke that would have graced the centre court at Wimbledon on men's final day. Not only did it have the same grace and power, it also accurately found its target. McAteer's tongue tasted the blood that filled up his mouth and felt the sharpness of the broken teeth. Egan then struck a blow that bounced off the side of McAteer's forehead. It knocked him to the floor and into a state of unconsciousness. When their victim regained his sense of time and place he found that Dillon and his companions had started to make use of the contents of the plastic bag.

His back was on the large wooden kitchen table. The dishes from the family's last meal had not been cleared but someone had just swept them on to the floor. McAteer could see that a good number of them were broken now and the remnants of the meal that they had contained lay over the already dirty linoleum. Electrical insulating tape had been placed over his mouth and prevented a rolled up handkerchief being spat out. He found that he could make only the most muted of sounds and tried to bring his hands up to remove the tape, but they would not comply. He had just enough play on his bonds to be able to look down and investigate this paralysis. He saw that each wrist had been fettered with a set of handcuffs to a table leg. His legs were being held tightly by Smith and Egan. A new plug was in the socket on the wall and McAteer noticed that it belonged to an extension lead. He let his eyes follow the cable. At the other end he saw Dillon holding an electric drill, the bit pointing to the ceiling. The eyes of the two men met and Dillon held the stare before switching on the power. As McAteer struggled in vain against his restraints, his tormentor let the drill achieve full speed. He then pressed it hard against McAteer's left knee cap. As he did, he informed his victim. ''This is for running away from the job we gave you. It'll be worse though if you entertain any thoughts about blabbing.''

    They could see that he was trying to scream but the sound was barely heard above the whir of the drill. McAteer heard a crunching noise, saw blood spurt into the air and then he passed out again. When he had finished, Dillon instructed his henchmen to retrieve the handcuffs and take the gag off before his victim choked. Then he tipped the table until he had achieved a sufficient angle for the body to fall to the floor. As they left the house, they could hear the sound of children crying in one of the other rooms.

Mrs McAteer was brushed aside as they passed her, ignoring the deluge of questions as to why they had come and what they had done. Just before Dillon took his final step out of the house he heard her screech.

"You fucking Orange bastards."

He smiled at the epithets and decided for these, he would wait a few moments longer. He watched her go into the kitchen and listened to her call out, "Oh my God! What have they fucking done to ye." And then to one of the children, "Run to the phone box and get an ambulance - it's yir da."

During the early evening of that day Dillon called at the Sullivans' house. He noticed the curtains of the lounge being pulled back and someone observing him through the lace lining. A moment later Peter opened the door and beckoned him inside. They went straight into the lounge where Isabel was seated. Dillon remained standing and indicated that he couldn't stay for long. He had a copy of the current evening paper in his hand and addressing his question directly to Peter asked whether he had seen it. Peter picked up his copy of the "Evening Times", from a coffee table and indicated that as yet he had only read the headlines and the football stories on the back page.

"Turn to page 5, about half way down", instructed Dillon.

At the directed spot Peter found the passage to

which Dillon was referring. Isabel had come across and was reading over his shoulder. The report told how a Ronald McAteer of Larkhall, Lanarkshire had suffered horrific injuries after he had been assaulted in his own home earlier that day. The police were apparently as yet unable to interview the victim as he was still under sedation. The story then concluded with a paragraph quoting the investigating officer and to the effect that although he had no idea about the motive behind the attack Mr McAteer was known to have links with Protestant terrorist organisations in Northern Ireland.

"So it was the right guy", confirmed Peter."

"No doubt about it, my hearty!"

Peter had not heard this jovial form of address before. It caused him to note just how generally pleased with himself Dillon was looking. The appearance, however, did not lead Dillon into accepting a celebratory drink. Instead he explained his imminent departure in terms of a pressing business meeting as he turned towards the door. Peter indicated to his wife that he would see him out as he would like an opportunity to express his thanks. The two men stopped in the hall and Peter said "Look Dillon I'd be a liar if I said that I was totally happy about what you did today, but as I said the other night I was pretty scared. So if you sorted that out for me I really do owe you a favour. I was wondering if your organisation might accept this little donation from me."

He held out five ten pound notes which Dillon took. As he transferred them to his wallet he said, "Thanks for these Peter I assure you that they will be put to good use." Then he continued, "As far as I'm concerned that's us all square and I'm pretty sure that you won't be bothered by that mob again. But you know that business across the water isn't going to go away. That peace movement will fizzle out and the men of violence on both sides will carry on. I suspect that the ''Derry Bar'' might get its fair share of the attacks that will be carried out on the, the..."

He had come to an abrupt halt. It was though his vocabulary was inadequate. He seemed to be searching for words. Then he found them and continued. "The island of Britain, or at the very least you will get headbangers like that last mob coming along and looking for trouble."

Peter nodded. He had already concluded that a scenario such that Dillon was now painting was indeed a very real possibility. He had also reckoned that another incident similar to the one that occurred that Saturday afternoon might actually frighten some customers away and lose him business. He did not get a chance to articulate that opinion as Dillon continued, "The thing is Peter, as things stand at the moment I won't be able to help again. I got that wee wrist slap from my boss. He wasn't too pleased about calling in favours from the police and using up resources to help somebody that isn't one of us."

"Oh, but you know that I'm right with you. Remember what I said about arming the Bogside. Won't that fifty quid convince your boss?"

"No it won't, Peter. It's not enough. He's a fervent adherent of the old maxim that whoever is not with us, is by definition, against us. We're talking here not just about donations, about money. We're talking here about commitment."

"Commitment", repeated Peter, "what are you looking for?"

"Just what I asked you for a few months ago. Your say-so to organise regular collections in the pub."

"So how would that work?"

"Dead easy, maybe twice a month, probably at the end of one of your sing-song nights somebody would announce that a wee collection is being taken up to help the struggle in the six counties. And then maybe Sean or one of the other boys would pass a bucket around. I'd come along at the end of the night and pick it up. Nothing to it really You'd not be alone either. It's happening in quite a few places, you know."

"O.K. We'll give it a try."

Dillon smiled and grabbed Peter's hand to shake it. "That's great, Peter I always thought you'd come on board. How about kicking it off next Friday? That would be the best night, wouldn't it?

I'll come along and maybe do a wee introduction, if you like.''

Peter nodded and forced himself to join in Dillon's smile. The two men said goodnight and Dillon almost skipped back to his car, satisfied with the accomplishments of that day. Peter started his return to the lounge and his wife moved away from the back of the door and reclaimed her seat.

Chapter 5

Public houses were then prevented by law from selling alcohol between 2-30 and 5 o'clock in the afternoon. Peter used these hours to go home and freshen up for the evening. As he drove the few miles that afternoon, he wondered how his customers would receive Dillon's appeal that evening. He brought his car to a halt in the driveway and noticed signs of occupancy which both puzzled and perplexed him. The storm doors were open and a light shone in the hall. The initial relief he acquired from noticing Isabel's car sitting in the drive would soon dissipate.

She was always out when he returned in the afternoon and he had come to enjoy this time of solitude. He traced her voice to the bathroom but found that the door was locked. He conveyed his irritation by persisting to turn the handle in spite of this. She shouted through the door that she would vacate that room shortly and advised that should he be so desperate to use it, he should avail himself of the downstairs bathroom. His main source of frustration was not the postponement of his toiletries but rather the imposed delay in ascertaining why on the precise day he needed solitude to collect his thoughts, his wife should be at home. Eventually she came down to join him in the kitchen. He asked her if she would like a cup of coffee but she declined. No other information was forthcoming from her and he managed to contain the erupting curiosity for only a few minutes.

"Something special happening, today?"

"No. Why do you ask?"

"Well it's very rare to see you home at this time."

Then he noticed the heavy make up on her eyes and lips and added.

"And it looks as though your preparing to go out."

"I thought I'd come to the shop tonight. Maybe even give you a hand behind the bar."

"Eh?", Peter questioned whether he had heard her accurately, but when there was obviously going to be no correction, he continued. "You've never worked behind a bar in your life before. You wouldn't know where to start. What's brought this on?" She decided to address his points in the order that he had raised them. "You don't know for sure that I've never worked in a pub before. I had a life before I met you, you know. Anyway, why shouldn't I come along if I want to? Remember your marriage vows. "With my worldly goods I thee endow", So half of it's mine anyway. Besides, wouldn't your regulars like to see the boss's wife? You wouldn't be ashamed of me, would you now, Peter?"

She was laughing now, so obviously enjoying teasing him. Peter had not before emotionally tackled the idea that his marriage meant giving up half of

59

his father's legacy, but he did not feel that this would be an appropriate time to dissect that notion. He brought up another more immediate concern.

"Look, tonight's the night that John Dillon is coming along to start a collection for the I.R.A. It's just possible that there might be a bit of trouble. I hope not but it would be better if you left your visit to the shop until another night."

"The Officials or the Provos?", she asked. The question was greeted by only a bemused expression. Isabel expanded, "Which bit of the I.R.A. does he collect for?"

Peter was unsure of his ground; it seemed to quake beneath him. He did have a vague knowledge of the recent schism within that organisation but it was not sufficiently detailed to enter into any debate about it. He also suspected that the question was not really a point of clarification but rather an attempt to make him uneasy at his lack of understanding of current affairs.

"What has that got to do with anything?"

"I'm just curious exactly who Mr Dillon represents. They have just split, didn't you know? It seems to me that I should come along tonight in case you put your foot in it." Isabel would not be dissuaded.

Arthur Reilley started the singing off as usual. Around nine o'clock Dillon came in, still in that same green Barbour jacket. He was immediately taken aback when he noticed Isabel behind the bar. Her green dress was cut so low that eyes were automatically drawn to her cleavage. It complemented her flaming red hair and she had been admired, if not explicitly, by all the males in the pub. She smiled at Dillon, not just a smile of recognition but a gesture that hinted at a deeper type of bond between them. She watched Dillon as he went across to the M.C. and quietly spoke to him.

Peter finished serving some drinks and then he came up to the two men as they talked, "All set, then?" he said trying to ensure that there was a smile on his face for Dillon to notice.

"Yes. Ready to go. I've just arranged with Arthur that I'd do a song first. It gives me an opportunity to introduce the collection."

Arthur Reilley's voice took over as the previous singer left the microphone. "Ladies and Gentlemen, I want you to give a big welcome to a new singer in the "Derry Bar" - Johnny Dillon. You'll recognise from the dulcet tones that he's a bit more recently arrived from the old country than most of us." Arthur thought that adding the "ny" sound gave Dillon a sort of Country and Western appeal, but Dillon scowled when he heard it. He had last been called "Johnny" at Primary School and regarded that period of his life as being behind him now. His hands were raised to acknowledge the applause, however, when he jumped up on the small dais that acted as a stage.

He sang.

> "There was a wild colonial boy,
> Jack Dougan was his name.
> He was born and bred in Ireland.
> In a town called Castlemaine......"

The crowd knew this song well and started to accompany Dillon. Quickly it appreciated though, just what a fine voice he had and content to listen left the singing completely to him. They applauded rapturously when he had finished. Dillon nodded and smiled his appreciation. Somebody was shouting for him to sing again but instead he held up his hand to indicate that he wanted to say something. When the noise subsided to a level with which he felt comfortable, he spoke to his audience.

"Thanks very much, folks I'd like to take up just a few minutes of your drinking time and then I'll be delighted to give you another song."

Only a small number continued their conversations and these were asked to be quiet by the others. When he had everybody's attention he continued.

"That was a wee song about one of Ireland's sons. But, you know, Ireland really has thirty two children whom she loves dearly; like any parent loves their children; like Jack Dougan's parents loved him. Now as you know six of these children have been cruelly taken from her. Antrim, Armagh, Derry, Down, Fermanagh and Tyrone are all held by an army of occupation. No Irishman or woman should be able to rest until they are returned to her. I want to assure you, friends, that they will be returned. Maybe not tomorrow, perhaps not even the next day, but surely they will be brought back into the fold. Then and only then will we be a nation once again.''

This last phrase registered with some of the audience and they interrupted Dillon's flow by clapping loudly. He acknowledged the support before proceeding ''Thanks. You know I was born and brought up just off the Falls Road in Belfast. What, a hundred miles or so from here? And yet I can tell you all that I feel at home here. I know that I'm amongst friends. Not just my friends but friends of old Ireland as well. Now these fools in the Dail are not going to do anything so it's up to folk like you and me to help these six children. I know that if it was possible we'd all march over there and tear down the castle dark at Stormont brick by brick. We can't do that but what we can do is help others do it. Fortunately there are still men and women who are willing to risk their lives and take up arms in the struggle for a united Ireland. But they need your help to buy the guns and the bullets. You know the talking's over. So I'm asking you to dig deep into not just your hearts tonight, but your pockets as well. A united Ireland will never be defeated again.''

He had at last reached the critical point of his speech and Peter looked anxiously around to see whether he could detect any antipathy to the request. They all seemed to be cheering, however, and some were already reaching for wallets or purses. Dillon raised his hands, one of which contained a yellow plastic bucket, in the air and gave the details of the method of contributing.

"Your man Sean, whom you all know, is going to go round and amongst you with this here bucket. I want you to throw in whatever you can afford. Mind, it's a paper collection, I expect here. So I don't want to hear any clinking of buttons or coins. In the meantime, I'll sing you a favourite of mine. You all know it I'm sure. It's called 'The Soldier's Song'."

As he left, people were clapping his back and shaking his hand. All he could feel, though, was Isabel's incessant stare burn into his face. He glanced at her only once and when he did he saw her tongue lick the exaggerated red lips. He went and stood beside Peter until Sean came over, then took a plastic bag out of his pocket and, without counting, emptied the money from the bucket into it.

"Looks like you have got a generous crowd in tonight, Peter I'll come back in a fortnight and do the same again."

Peter noted that this was given as information rather than being presented as a request. He wondered whether he should raise this point but Dillon was already saying goodnight to practically everyone in the pub and departed shortly afterwards.

Chapter 6

"You are a very elusive man, Mr Dillon. I've tried five times this week to reach you."

There was a silence for the briefest of moments as Dillon tried to locate in his mind the owner of the voice at the other end of the telephone line. Then recognition came to him and he responded.

"Then you are a very persistent lady, Mrs Sullivan. Now that you've got me what can I do for you."

"You can take me out for lunch."

"And a very direct lady, as well. It's my guess that when a lady asks me to take her out for lunch as opposed to joining her, she generally means that her husband isn't coming along. Would that be the case here I wonder?"

This did not sound like the diffident Mr Dillon that Isabel had teased previously but she relished this approach. She wondered whether the lack of face to face contact gave him a new confidence.

"You can wonder what you like Mr Dillon. Perhaps I can leave you to make a reservation somewhere reasonably discreet, but you will only require to book a table for two."

"A table for two it is then."

They arranged that Dillon would collect her from the bottom of her drive at noon the following day. She was waiting when he arrived.

"Where are we going Mr Dillon?" enquired Isabel as she let herself into his car. She noted that the Barbour jacket had been left behind.

"Do you know "The Vintners" on Clyde Street just facing the river, Mrs Sullivan?"

"I think if we are going out for lunch together, you should call me Isabel."

"Fine, perhaps you would drop the 'Mr'."

"Suits me, Dillon. Isn't "The Vintners" a bar for homosexuals."

Dillon had started driving. The idea of Isabel calling him only by his surname seemed to add to the notion he was gathering of her having a sexual power over him, but he restrained this thought and addressed her query.

"The bar has got that reputation but there's a restaurant upstairs that I think is very good."

Isabel thought so too at the end of their meal. It was not at all ostentatious but presented a relaxed, friendly atmosphere. A casually dressed man, who greeted Dillon by name, showed them to a small discreet booth in the corner of the restaurant. He took Isabel's expensive coat and allowed Dillon to see that she was wearing a skirt that covered, when she was standing, only half of her thigh. It displayed legs that were at once muscular and sensual.

"Do you think I'm too old to wear a skirt like this, Dillon?"

Dillon was conscious that their waiter was well

within earshot and would have preferred to have this conversation in more private surroundings. He replied succinctly and in a manner less flattering than that for which Isabel had hoped.

"Not at all. You're as young as you feel."

"Peter says it's like mutton dressed up as lamb, but his taste in everything is in his backside."

Dillon let the remark pass and pulled out the seat for her. A table covered with a starched linen cloth had been laid for two. Jutting out from the wall on either side of the booth were panels of dark polished wood, each of which held a rather ornate stained glass window. Isabel who dined out fairly frequently in the recognised better restaurants was also impressed by the food which she complemented with a full bottle of reasonable claret, save for the one half glass that Dillon took for himself. They discussed Peter at some length over their meal. Dillon took care not to make perjorative comments about him, but Isabel displayed no such restraint. She described how he lived still in the shadow of his father. When he had a success in business or even when the pub had a particularly good night's takings, Peter would talk about how he 'was proving the old man wrong' about his business acumen.

Dillon interjected in what he believed to be the most diplomatic manner. "Every marriage, they tell me has its problems."

"We're not talking about problems. Do you

know Tolstoy's famous opening line in 'Anna Karenina'?"

He thought for a moment or two and then said, "Something about 'All happy families resembling one another, but each unhappy family is unhappy in its own fashion'."

"Very good! Top of the class. That's near enough. Well our particular fashion is that, living or dead, old man Sullivan's approval remains the most important thing in our house."

She continued to tell Dillon that she and Peter had tried for some time for children but she did not conceive. Shortly before old Sullivan died they had sought some medical help. They duly learned that Peter had a very low sperm count and that this was the most probable cause of their failure. For some reason, inexplicable to Isabel, Peter had informed his father of this revelation. He did not get a sympathetic response. Old Sullivan had started by laughing at him and saying he 'could only fire blanks' and then had become angry. He went on about wanting to ensure that the business would stay in the family and that he would be contacting his solicitor to see if he could bequeath it directly to his first grandchild, although at that time none of Peter's brothers or sisters had any offspring. Sullivan died before he could make any specific enquiries in this direction and Peter never discussed it with anyone except Isabel.

They lingered over their coffee and Dillon felt the restaurant emptying around them. They would have to leave soon. This precipitated an urgency in Dillon's voice as he asked the question that he had been holding in his head throughout the whole meal.

"Why did you suggest lunch together today?"

"Who knows? It's not everyday you meet somebody that carries a gun or dispenses his own form of justice. Maybe I was impressed by your speech. You're an interesting man, Dillon."

"'Interesting' is the word you keep to use when you can't really think of anything complimentary to say. It's a cold praise."

"You think so? Where do you stay?"

"In a flat in the West End. Up a close." He smiled at his use of his last word. He had only heard tenement buildings described in this fashion since his arrival in Glasgow and then he remembered the occasion when his companion's husband had introduced their house in Burnside. "The stairs are on the outside."

Isabel was puzzled but easily managed to ignore this remark and the sarcasm that carried it to continue with her investigation.

"By yourself?"

"No, as a matter of fact I share it with a colleague of mine, Gerry Timms. He's in the same line of work as me and it goes without saying, he's employed by the same firm."

"Is he there this afternoon?"

Dillon was becoming impatient with the barrage of questions.

"Look, what are all these questions about."

"Just tell me, is he in this afternoon?"

"If you really must know, he's in Belfast just now. He won't be back until next week."

"Where about is this flat?"

The irritation now transferred quite clearly to the tone of his voice.

"It's not customary in my job to be giving away my address to relative strangers."

"Oh for God's sake, shut up Dillon. I'm about to offer you sex this afternoon. Are you interested or do you belong to the group that frequents the downstairs bar?"

"No, Mrs Sullivan, of all the little idiosyncrasies that I've collected in my life, that isn't one of them."

They left for Dillon's flat and went straight to lie on top of the bed. They kissed and he placed his hand on top of her breast. She stroked the back of his head and pulled his hair until she was on top of him. He understood the signs of encouragement emanating from her passion and enthusiasm. He opened the buttons at the front of her dress. Her tongue was in his mouth, pushing his tongue back and emphasising the mutuality of the excitement. It was exhorting him to further arousal. His hand released a breast from the confines of her bra and he shifted his mouth to kiss it. The nipple was standing proud and erect and Dillon let his tongue circumscribe it before gently squeezing it with his teeth. They both looked at it and she smiled before putting both arms around him and squeezing tightly. She pulled him on top of her and could feel his penis hard. She unzipped his fly and her hand found its way through the front of his underpants to pull the skin of his penis down. He gave a little yelp of pain and pleasure and she gently cupped her hands to hold his testicles. He had followed her lead and although the elastic of both her tights and knickers clung tightly to hinder his access, he found he was able the squeeze his hand through. His fingers gently massaged the lips of her vagina and he felt it get more and more moist. She groaned and then she abruptly pushed him off.

"Get your clothes off, Dillon."

Dillon stood up and started to undress. She smiled when she noticed that he had a temporary difficulty getting his underpants over his erect penis. She let him stand naked in front of her as she undressed. Then she lifted her hand bag and took out a packet of condoms. Dillon saw her put it on the bedside table as she pulled back the covers to get in, and asked.

"Do you always carry these things or did you buy them for today?"

"I got them this morning but I hadn't made up

my mind then whether or not I was going to use them. So don't flatter yourself too much."

She made a fist around his penis and moved the skin up and down until it was as hard as before and then slipped the condom on for him. The hair at the back of her head was pulled tightly as he manoeuvred himself on top of her.

Their lovemaking was disappointing for both of them. He came before she climaxed and he knew it through the vacuous look on her face. He rolled over and waited a few moments before speaking.

"I'm sorry."

"You don't need to apologise. It'll be better the next time."

"You're telling me that there will be a next time?"

"If you'd like that."

"I'd like it a lot, Isabel."

She kissed him on the cheek and he rubbed his hand over her face. She was curious.

"When was the last time you were with a woman?"

"Someone I cared about, that was a long time ago. My wife was killed way back in '62. The last I.R.A. campaign."

Isabel noticed that he was struggling to maintain his composure, but her curiosity had not been sated.

"What? You mean the I.R.A. killed your wife?

Wasn't she on their side?" Dillon was visibly trembling as he answered.

"Yes, of course she was. But accidents happen in war, you know nineteen people were killed in the last campaign. It went on for six years. It was inevitable that a few things happened that shouldn't have."

The emotion had disappeared and he had related the facts as though he were answering a question in some diabolical quiz.

Isabel wondered whether his wife had been accidentally shot or bombed. It even occurred to her that she might have been planting or making a bomb when it exploded. Before she could seek further details, though, Dillon spoke again and the words rested incongruously with the recently displayed detachment.

"I'm afraid it's still pretty painful for me. Do you mind if we skip that bit?"

"O.K. But you've really never been with a woman in what - nearly eight years?"

"Well if it's the time for the honest truth there have been one or two ladies of the night that I've met around Blythswood Square."

"You mean prostitutes?"

"Yeah. Does that disgust you?"

"No, it doesn't disgust me at all. Do you know Dali's painting 'Christ of St. John of the Cross'."

Dillon tried hard to see how that question fitted in with the rest of their conversation but failed. He noticed though she was now putting on her clothes in preparation for her departure.

He replied. "The one hanging up in the Kelvingrove Art Gallery? Salvador Dali's painting."

"That's the only Dali that I know and as far as I believe that's the only 'Saint John of the Cross' that he painted. I'll meet you there at noon next Friday. The neighbours would have a field day if they saw you coming to collect me again. You don't need to see me out. I'll pick up a taxi on Byres Road."

Neither of those two statements of intent seemed open to negotiation.

Chapter 7

When the young Dillon established the romantic nature of his relationship with the girl who would in time become his wife, at a dance in Limivaddy, the prospect of their next meeting held neither excitement nor fear for him. He recalled that he had been left cold when he thought about their date. They had chummed along in the same group of gauche teenagers and it was almost expected that they would start to see each other in a way that would lead to more adult matters. This sterility of feelings was most certainly not the case when he anticipated his meeting with Isabel. The days intervening between their meeting and that Friday seemed interminably long.

He grew angry with himself. Tantalising expectations should be confined to the first flushes of romantic awakenings. That they should be present in the mind of a mature man challenged the very self image that Dillon held of himself. There was also in his consciousness the idea that before the assignation would occur, he must first meet the cuckold.

The second collection in the "Derry Bar" was as successful as the first, with only minimal encouragement being required to persuade the sympathetic crowd to give generously to the cause.

Dillon came along as arranged in the middle of the evening. Relief and disappointment vied with each other for predominance when he realised that

Isabel was not present on this occasion. Their struggle would have continued had Dillon's mind not been diverted by the shouts from those who had heard him singing before. Arthur Reilley delivered a brief introduction and Dillon answered their call with a rendition of 'Forty Shades of Green', before he sought out Peter to congratulate him on the amount of money that had been raised.

"That's really great my hearty. The folks across the water will be really pleased with the support that you're drumming up for us here. I take it that this will be a regular event in future. I'll come along every second Friday and pick up whatever we've got in the bucket. That sound OK to you?"

It seemed to Peter that whether or not it sounded OK to him or not was completely irrelevant. There was not an option to stop the process at this point. The customers seemed to approve, Dillon was pressing for it and whatever protection his organisation offered was dependent on the collections continuing. The very birth of the authorisation of these collections had granted it a power and significance of its own. Peter simply nodded his head in agreement to the question. Dillon continued, "The other thing that you might like to think about, Peter, is Irish poetry readings. Do you know any, Yeats - William Butler. What a man. A great Irish patriot and one of the world's best poets without a doubt."

Peter was sure that this suggestion was being

made with Dillon's tongue firmly pressed into his cheek, but then heard him start to quote.

"Now and in time to be
Wherever green is worn
All changed, changed utterly
A terrible beauty is born."

"Easter 1916, Peter. What do you think the terrible beauty is?"

Not only was the landlord bemused at this enquiry, he was also embarrassed. It would be a source of some teasing from his regulars were one of them to overhear this discussion about poetry. To them the rhyme was the medium of the toilet wall.
"Haven't a clue, but I'm not too sure that. . . ." Dillon abruptly cut him off.

"We are, we are that 'terrible beauty' born. People like you and me who are dedicated to making Ireland a nation once again."

"Oh, right. Very good. Look John, I know the folk that come in here. This poetry business isn't such a good idea if you don't mind me saying so. A good sing song, that's what they really like. Songs where they can all join in."

Dillon looked disappointed, but managed the beginnings of a smile as he responded.

"Fine. No problem. Just a thought. The other thing that has worked elsewhere is Irish dancing. One of your customers is bound to know a few kids who have learned to do a proper jig and that's always good entertainment before a collection."

"Aye that sounds a bit more reasonable. Leave it with me and I'll give it some thought", came the unconvincing response.

It would have taken Dillon no more than twenty minutes to walk from his flat to the Kelvingrove Art Gallery, but he was unsure what Isabel might wish to do after they met. Consequently he decided to take his car. He was not unduly impeded by any traffic lights and arrived almost half an hour early. He justified his timing by the notion that he might have difficulty in locating the actual painting, but again this presented no problems. He was then surprised to see that Isabel was already there and waiting for him on a long wooden bench. She was staring intently at the image of Christ who had risen above the world and was looking down at the mortal fishermen below. The Cross seemed to tilt more and more towards Dillon as he approached and the unsupported body upon it hung alarmingly forward showing the top of the head. Just as Isabel's face was turned away from him, so also was he denied the face of the figure in the picture. Dillon found himself being brought to a halt by this effect, just behind Isabel. He reached out and let his palm rest momentarily on her shoulder. She was startled by the interruption.

"Hello there Isabel. I thought that I'd be too early to find you here yet."

"Hi Dillon. I wondered whether you would

come or not. This painting got me into terrible trouble when I was about fourteen or so. Did you know that?''

The head shake did not indicate how obvious Dillon thought his ignorance of this event should be. As he sat down beside her he wanted to ask why she had doubts about his keeping the appointment, but Isabel continued to tell her story.

''I went to a Catholic girls school not very far from here called Notre Dame. It was pretty strict in those days and was run by nuns and priests. One day we came to this Art Gallery with one of our priests. I can still see him clearly. Father Sorley was his name. Anyway he was explaining this picture to us. It's all about sin and redemption of the soul, you know. Father Sorley said that the angle of the body on the cross makes it look like a crucifix being presented to the lips of someone on his death bed. It means that the effect of the crucifixion, the bit about Christ taking away the sins of mankind can go on forever. He said that this act of forgiveness was so great that it couldn't be repeated or even added to. I then asked him what was the point of going to confession. He went puce. He started to shout at me and the whole class was marched back to school. I was given six of the strap by one of the nuns and told to go away and pray for forgiveness.''

''So have you remained a practising Catholic, then?''

"Yeah, I suppose I have nominally at least." Isabel failed to see her companion bite his bottom lip and she carried on.

"I reckon I'll stay a Catholic until I work this guilt thing out. Is it a crutch that lets you stand up in this world or is it the scythe that cuts your feet from under you? It's one of the two reasons that Peter and I don't get a divorce."

"What's the other reason?"

"Can't you guess Dillon? It would be too painful for that bastard to give up the half of the business that I would demand. I kept house while he went out and I want my share."

"Do you think that the reason he'd be reluctant to let it go is because of that little chat with his dad that you told me about last time."

Isabel looked at him for a moment before replying, "It might be, then again maybe its just greed. What do you think?"

Dillon thought that the more pedantic explanation of avarice to be more probable but decided to hold his own counsel. Isabel threw another question at him. "Do you still go to Confession?"

She noticed the squirm in his seat as he replied.

"No. Not any longer. Now what do you want to do with the afternoon?"

They decided that they would have a coffee and a sandwich in the Art Gallery's tea room and then return to the flat.

"I'd better tell you right now that Gerry is back from Belfast", said Dillon.

"So does that mean there are problems taking me back there?"

"No, you're all right. If we want to be alone we can go into my room. The only thing is I really would not want Gerry to find out who you are. If it got back to Belfast that I was having an affair with one of my, my....", he hesitated, obviously having difficulty with the choice of an appropriate noun "my clients, then I would be in hot water."

Isabel's first thought was that there was an irony in the notion that terrorists should try to occupy this moral high ground, but then guessed that it may have something to do with security. Other thoughts had entered her head and she pursued their discussion with a cutting sarcastic edge to her voice.

"So I've just learned three things. Gerry tells stories out of school. Peter is a client of yours and we are having an affair."

"I'm sorry. 'Affair' was the only word I could think of. Perhaps that's a bit presumptuous of me."

"Oh for God's sake lighten up a bit Dillon. Don't take everything I say too seriously. The word; 'affair' just conjures up in my mind something a bit more long term. Our relationship is more, what's the word, ephemeral? Carpe Diem, eh, Dillon?"

After their lunch Isabel decided that she would like to stroll through the park that adjoined the Art

Gallery. She brushed aside Dillon's objections that he had brought his car precisely to facilitate the return journey to his flat and told him that when she had to go he could use her taxi to collect the car. They walked into the park and climbed to the flagpole. They stopped there and took in the vista of the city. In the afternoon light, the towers of the University dominated the foreground but Dillon strained to see beyond them. He clenched the railings and spoke without looking at Isabel.

"Glasgow is really a lot like Belfast. I think that's the reason I like the place so much. See the cranes standing on the Clyde, over there. Every time I see them they remind me about the time I spent at my grandparents. Even though they don't move any more they make me think about Belfast Lough and the yards there. Granddad used to stay just outside Harland and Wolffe but never got a job in the yards. Even now when I go back to Belfast I see these two big yellow cranes dominating the skyline, you can see them from all over the place, and they just start to speak to me. They tell me exactly where I used to stay and then they start to tell me what happened."

Isabel had moved around to observe Dillon's expressions but had difficulty interpreting them at first, "Why did you stay with your grandparents?", she enquired.

"It's far too long a story to go into just now."

Isabel would not allow him to change the subject at that point. She tenaciously encouraged him to give her at least a hint as to the content of this family drama.

"Well, basically it was because my father sometimes hit my mother and one day he went a bit too far. So she collected my brother and I and left when he was out of the house. That's when we went to stay with Gran and Pop."

She now could clearly recognise the expressions as pain but was driven by a force inside her to continue her torment. She wondered whether she was taking pleasure at inflicting suffering because the victim was a man who had clearly demonstrated his ability to do precisely the same to others.

"It all makes sense now", she said. "Your father had a booze problem and that's why you steer clear of the drink, is it?"

"You must be getting me confused with someone else Isabel. Liquor wasn't the issue. My old man hardly touched a drop. Their main problem was that they had a mixed marriage. He was a Proddy and she was a Catholic; and in all of the worst places in the world to have a mixed marriage it's fair hard to top Belfast. Mammy started off by saying that she would turn, but her family and the Church wouldn't allow her to do that. She stayed with my father for fourteen years but in all that time in her heart of hearts she was always Catholic, Irish and Republican. My brother and me used to lie awake at night listening to their fights. She would swear at him, he'd call her a Fenian bitch, she would say something else and then he would belt her one. Not a pretty thing to have to experience. When I was about thirteen she decided enough was enough and upped and left him. That's how I ended up staying at Pop's, but I learned that I couldn't spend my life with someone who didn't share my religion or my political beliefs. That was a hard lesson for a young boy, Isabel."

He nodded his head as though to emphasise this point to himself. Isabel was about to chide him for being a bigot but noticed the vehemence in his voice. She asked "So how do you feel about it now?"

The grin spread across of his face. "How do I feel this very minute?"

That was not the question that Isabel had put but she was glad to move the discussion forward and the grin seductively invited her to play his game.

"Yes, now. This very minute."

"Randy as hell."

The first thing Isabel noticed when they returned to the flat was how untidy it had become since her last visit. A number of unwashed dishes cluttered the kitchen, newspapers had been left unfolded on the lounge floor and a small bundle of clothes on their way to the washing machine had been deposited in the hall. Dillon started to apologise profusely but he was stopped with her protestations that the condition of the flat was of no importance at all.

"So where is the mysterious Mr Timms?", she enquired.

"Doesn't seem to be any sign of him. He must have gone out. Let's take a coffee into my bedroom and maybe I'll be able to skip the introductions."

Isabel again sat on top of the bed and invited Dillon to join her. He came up from behind and started to kiss the back of her neck.

"Talk to me first, Dillon. I'm not ready yet."

"Christ, Isabel. What do you want me to say. I've been wanting you all week. I can only think about kissing you and rubbing you and....."

Isabel had been rolling her head backwards and forwards. She was obviously enjoying his attentions but wanted more. She interrupted him at that point.

"Yes, that's nice. I want you to do all those things to me and more but tell me now what you like."

Had this conversation been overheard, it would have been soon realised that Dillon's embarrassment had started to cause him difficulties. He started to speak, then stuttered and then said something that was quite inaudible to Isabel's ears. She gently cajoled him to articulate his desires.

"Come on, tell me Dillon, what is it that you like about me. What bits of me turn you on?"

Beads of sweat broke loose on his forehead as

Isabel unbuttoned the front of his shirt and ran her open palm along the top of his trousers.

"It isn't any bit of you that gives me the hots. It's all of you. I find you a very powerful lady. You order me about. You call me by my surname. You take charge. That turns me on."

He became aware that the short staccato sentences that he was using reflected the pattern of his breathing. He gulped and tried to regain the composure that was rapidly slipping away from him.

"No-one's ever done that to me before. I like it. Is that strange?"

She ignored the question and barked at him.

"That's your bag is it, you dirty little pervert. Well we can certainly use and abuse you if you like. Is that what you would like? Answer me now."

She had shouted this last command at him. Dillon was at first taken by surprise and then caught in the vice of anxiety and excitement. He was anxious lest his flatmate had returned and was being disturbed by the noise but was becoming more and more excitable as Isabel exercised her dominance over him. Intellectually he recognised that they were playing a game, but emotionally and physically he was living out a fantasy. All of a sudden it became of no importance whether Gerry heard. At the most he reckoned there would be unidentifiable sounds coming from the bedroom.

"Yes Isabel. Yes I do want you to abuse me.

I want you to do whatever you like to me. I'll do whatever you tell me.''

''Good boy. You can call me 'madam'. Now I want you to strip and kneel in front of me I'm going to inspect you to see if you want me enough. Do you understand?''

When he was naked and kneeling Isabel walked around him. She stood behind him and said, ''Madam should tie you up and take her pleasure from you.''

It had been a casual remark made in the spirit of the fantasy. She was surprised when Dillon told her that he had two sets of handcuffs in the top drawer of his cabinet. Her knowledge of Dillon's activities already extended to the point where she knew that it would not be prudent to enquire why he had these instruments or for what purpose they had been previously employed. She ordered him to lie on the bed and then attached one handcuff of each set to each of his wrists. When the other handcuff was secured to a bedpost she started to taunt him about not being able to touch her. She made admiring remarks about his erect penis and then sat astride him. She massaged herself with Dillon's penis until she climaxed. Dillon ejaculated almost immediately afterwards.

Isabel fell on top of him and they lay together for a few minutes listening to the sound of each other breathing and the rhythm of their heartbeats. Dillon was the first to put his thoughts into words.

'This sounds pretty corny, almost the sort of thing I would expect to hear in a cliché ridden film, but that was really great. Better than any sex that I've had to pay for.''

"It should be Dillon. I had to work damn hard to get pleasure out of you. I wasn't going to go home high and dry like last week."

Isabel could see immediately the puzzlement and hurt on his face that this reply had caused. The remark had not been appreciated as the jest it was meant to be. She moved quickly to make reparations.

"I'm kidding you. It felt really good to me too. I have to be going now but I hope we can do that again."

After Dillon was released and they had dressed, they went through to the lounge to phone for a taxi. It would allow Dillon to collect his car and then take Isabel home. They were both taken aback to see a tall man sitting on the sofa watching television. He turned around slowly as the couple entered. Isabel noticed that he was in stocking soles and had a newspaper covering his lap. He deliberately let the journal fall to the floor and stood up. He smiled a lascivious leer at Isabel and then turned to look inquisitively at Dillon, whose face had turned a very bright shade of red.

"Gerry, I didn't hear you come home."

"Really! You must have been busy with something else. I've been here for a while.''

Isabel decided that she did not like this person and felt uncomfortable with the way that he stared at her. Her companion interpreted the glances at Isabel as a cue for an introduction.

''Gerry this is a friend of mine, Isabel.....'', he was still blushing and a slight stammer crept into his voice, ''...Isabel Armstrong.''

She shot a glance of surprise at the sound of the unfamiliar name, but he did not even bother to look in her direction before continuing.

''Isabel, this is Gerry Timms, my good friend and,'' he had stopped and was looking around the room at the general signs of untidiness that Isabel had earlier noticed, ''and bad flatmate.''

The hand that Timms offered felt warm and sweaty. She withdrew hers as soon as politeness would allow and tried hard to stretch her lips into a gesture that could be taken as welcoming. As soon as the taxi peeped its horn Isabel made for the door, leaving Dillon to follow. Once inside the cab she asked why he had introduced her by the name 'Armstrong'.

''I'm sorry Isabel. It was just the first one that came into my head. I couldn't use 'Sullivan' in case he started to suspect that you might be THE Mrs Sullivan, that I know. I wasn't joking when I told you that the organisation would take a dim view if any of their representatives were to be fooling around with the wife of someone who was supporting them.

"Couldn't you have at least thought of a good Catholic name like O'Reilly or Donnelly." Isabel joked. He smiled in appreciation of her humour which allowed him to conceal the fleeting twinge of anxiety that he felt.

Chapter 8

The television screen relayed pictures of a church bell chiming. It then returned to scenes of a party in the studio. The sixties had finished and a new decade had begun. Peter Sullivan had closed the curtains of his front rooms lest any neighbours see a light and consider the idea of 'first footing' him. He did not want company. He still had three quarters or so of a bottle of whisky and it was his intention to finish it by himself. To celebrate vicariously the New Year by watching the revellers on television would be sufficient for him. He had had enough of talking.

Peter had closed the pub early the previous evening and had arranged with Isabel that they would go to a fellow publican's house to celebrate the coming of the 70's. When he arrived home to collect her he found her still dressed in the clothes she had worn in the house that day. He had enquired whether she would be changing and had been informed that she had no intention of accompanying him to that or indeed to any other party. Isabel continued to tell Peter that she no longer loved him and introduced the question of whether she ever had. It was not the realisation of this that stunned him, indeed he suspected that he already knew it, but having it openly stated to him left him shocked and incredulous. He finally stammered that he held it to be sacred that they had pledged in front of a priest to remain married till death. This meant, he adamantly told her, that he would not agree to a divorce and that she could leave him if she liked but he would ensure that his father's wishes were carried out and the business would remain solely in his family. He also brought to her attention that the house, although jointly owned, was the subject of a large mortgage and if sold would not at that time realise a lot of capital. To his surprise Isabel nodded her agreement to all of these points and added the suggestion that, since divorce was not a practical option in either religious or financial terms for either of them, they should live separate lives as far as sharing a home would permit.

He had been initially stunned by this suggestion and the callous pragmatism within it. He had known for years that his marriage was not satisfying for either party. He had followed the line of least resistance, however, and kept up a pretence, partly in his own mind, that matters would be resolved in the future. Now Isabel had forced him to address the reality of the situation and he found it painful. He asked her whether there was somebody else around for her. She tried at first to ignore this question but when he persisted she responded that if there was she would have been seeking a divorce. She thought though of Dillon as she delivered this denial. She then proceeded to inform him that they were to have separate bedrooms and that she had consequently prepared the spare room for him.

He became angry that she could deliver this verdict on his manner of living and on his future in such a nonchalant manner. He speculated that she must have spent days planning this manoeuvre. He went to hit her but she screamed at him and he refrained. As he lowered his hand he started to cry and asked her whether it was because he was unable to give her children.

His father had told him that this would lead to trouble, he informed her. Isabel shook her head incredulously as she listened to John Sullivan pontificate from the grave on the difficulties in her relationship with her husband. She did not respond but merely retired to the room that would now be hers and hers alone. Her husband watched her leave. He knew that her decision was not merely the result of a capricious whim; he did not realise though that they would never resume the intimacy of their previous relationship.

Peter found an unopened bottle of whisky, sat in front of the television set and wondered what the new decade would bring.

Chapter 9

Dillon continued to visit the "Derry Bar" every second Friday. The initial enthusiasm of the clientele, however, to contribute waned after six months or so. One evening the collector lingered a little bit longer than usual.

"Not rushing away tonight, John?", Arthur Reilley had enquired.

"Perhaps you'll give us a song."

"Maybe, Arthur. I just need to have a word with Mr Sullivan about a little business matter, first."

Eventually he caught Peter's attention and Dillon summoned him over to him with a wave of his hand.

"Yes, John, what can I do for you?"

"Can we have a little chat in private?"

"Well, there's not a lot of places behind the bar that's private, unless we go down the cellar."

"No, I tell you what Peter, let's go outside and sit in my car."

Peter felt very uncomfortable about giving up a territorial advantage but Dillon was staring hard at him and inviting him with a sweep of his hand towards the door. The smile on his face said that he would regard it as churlish to refuse. Peter shouted to Sean that he would be back in a few minutes and then almost as an afterthought for his own safety, he informed him quite unnecessarily that he would be sitting in Mr Dillon's car.

"What is it John? I'm intrigued with the need for privacy?

"It's not a big deal really. I just think there are somethings that are best not discussed in earshot of the customers. The thing is the last few collections have been a bit light and you're a businessman yourself so you know how difficult accounting is when you are unsure of how much is coming in. So what I want to suggest is that you and I agree a figure, say £100, that we can count on. If the collection is a bit short one evening then you would make up the difference. That would make it so much easier to plan things for the future 'cause we would know precisely how much we could spend." Dillon hesitated, he could feel Peter squirming in his seat at the thought of this proposal. There was no response, however. This was left to Dillon to seek. He added abruptly. "If you didn't feel that you could manage that then I'm not sure I could continue to insure you."

At first Peter was offended that Dillon had spelled out such basic principles of budgeting as though he had been speaking to someone of limited intelligence. Then he considered the ramifications of the proposal and grew indignant.

"You're changing the goal posts once the game has started, now. The deal was that I would allow you to collect. There was nothing said about protection money. That's what you mean when you say 'insure' isn't it?''

"Peter, don't offend me please. I'm not talking about protection money as you put it. This is a purely voluntarily arrangement."

Dillon went on to explain that his organisation had limited resources to collect the donations and forge links with sympathetic audiences. He continued to tell Peter how he and his partner covered the whole of Scotland between them and that there already was a number of pubs and clubs willing to enter into the sort of arrangement that he had just outlined and then added in a harsher tone that it would only be good business sense to concentrate resources on these premises. Peter understood immediately the threat inherent in this conclusion. He felt trapped. It was against all his business instincts to pay for something for which he hadn't asked in the first place but he realised that even if he hadn't needed Dillon's protection services before, then the instigation of the collections and the concomitant association of the pub with an Irish republican organisation meant that he certainly needed them now.

"A ton is a fair whack, John. What about just leaving it at fifty?"

"Don't worry, Peter. Most times I get well over eighty so you're not going to be that much out of pocket at a hundred, and I suspect that there'll be quite a few occasions when we clear that amount no trouble at all". Peter's response was characterised by a tone of resignation.

"O.K. John. The hundred it is."

"Thanks a lot again Peter. You're a good man. The last time around though was really piss poor, I'm, afraid. That's forty five you owe me for tonight. I'll pick it up the next time I'm around."

When Peter returned to the pub Arthur Reilley enquired whether Dillon would be coming back as he had promised them a rendition.

"Don't think so, Arthur. I think Mr Dillon has got what he came for."

In fact Peter found himself making significant contributions almost every fortnight. The amount collected tended to be in direct proportion to the publicity given to the situation in Ulster. If some dramatic event, particularly if it reflected the perceived injustices towards the Catholic community or progressed the Republican cause, was reported in the national news in the preceding week then the collection was greater. It still though, very rarely reached the target amount. If the situation became relatively quiet and little news percolated into the papers or onto the television screen, then Peter found himself paying larger amounts out of his own pocket.

Each year, Dillon would suggest to Peter that the target amount should be increased to keep pace with inflation and each suggested increase was well above the inflationary rate that Peter heard quoted elsewhere. Peter continued to feel that the deeper he got into the relationship with Dillon the more difficult it was to extricate himself from it. Consequently he continued to pay more and more money. As the years passed this became more of a financial burden. He was grateful that he could still summon up humour to cope with Dillon's increased demands and asked him on a number of occasions whether there would be any security breaches if he declared these donations on his tax returns. The first time that Peter raised this query, Dillon smiled and then simply nodded his head at the subsequent identical enquiries.

Only a few collections did not require a subsidy to compensate the deficit . These were directly related to events in Northern Ireland.

In February 1971, the first British soldier was killed by the I.R.A. and the following Friday, the "Derry Bar" contained its biggest ever crowd. A number of them had brought along green, white and gold tricolours and these were waived in the air during the singing of certain Republican anthems. Peter remembered Dillon's quote 'a terrible beauty born'. He thought those words were an apt description of the product of his father's grand plan that he witnessed that evening.

In August of the same year, internment was introduced and then on the 30th of January 1972, thirteen civilians were shot down by the British army in the streets of Londonderry. That day was later known as 'Bloody Sunday' and became a catalyst for a great deal of latent support growing active on both sides of the Irish Sea. All of these events led not only to large crowds coming along to the next 'Irish Night' in the "Derry Bar", but also to donations large enough to allow Peter to escape making a personal contribution. The increased generosity of the patrons would last for a month or so after the event to which it was related and then, to the landlord's chagrin, the deficit would appear again and gradually grow larger.

Within a few years Peter's enforced contribution became a millstone around his neck. He cursed it but continued to pay.

Dillon and Isabel's relationship flourished during this time. They met almost every Friday afternoon. Generally they would meet for lunch and frequently return to the "Vintners"; then they would take a stroll in a park or visit either the Botanic Gardens or Kelvingrove Art Gallery. Occasionally they would go to the cinema, but they invariably ended their date by returning to Dillon's flat and confining themselves in his bedroom for an hour or so. Both of them looked forward to their love making sessions. They found themselves becoming more intimate outside the bedroom. They would clasp each other's hands as they strolled, they kissed when they met and Dillon became less conscious of doing so in public places and they both sought opportunities to put their arms around each other. In the bedroom, however, their relationship was characterised by a lack of repression. They discussed each other's sexual wishes and thoughts. Put aside were any inhibitions that would previously have hindered the exploration of these fantasies. In the main they comprised of Isabel assuming a dominant role and Dillon acting as her captive slave. Apart from the handcuffs various other accoutrements were employed. Isabel purchased a pair of black patent leather boots that would be pulled over her thighs and several pairs of fishnet stockings. They later bought a whip through a mail order catalogue. Over the months the scenarios developed and became more elaborate. On a relatively few number of occasions the theme would be changed and Dillon would act as a martinet schoolmaster and Isabel his wayward pupil. Several little plays were formulated and acted out in that bedroom, but they all shared the common denouement of Dillon and Isabel making love together.

It was not purely a physical relationship though, for they talked and enjoyed each other's company in this activity as well. They discussed films that had recently been released and their reviews, world events, the restaurants in which they ate and the galleries that they visited.

The "Derry Bar" was mentioned during their

first few meetings and Dillon would tell her that there were a number of similar Irish bars not just in Britain but also in places like Boston, New York and Sydney. He had never been to any of these cities but knew of people there who were doing the same sort of job as Timms and himself.

Isabel in turn told him the story of how James Sullivan had deliberately employed an Irish theme to rescue the business from the local recession it had faced. They would also talk on occasions about Peter. Dillon enquired whether he might be growing suspicious of their relationship and Isabel would assure him that Peter was not sufficiently interested in her to enquire how she used her time. She also confided to him the outline of the discussion that she and Peter had recently had, and about living separate lives within the same house.

"It's the only way I can hold onto a reasonable amount of money, and it doesn't really cause me any great hardship. He gets a lot of his meals at the pub and washing and ironing a few shirts are the only demands that he makes on me now."

"Doesn't he want to touch you?"

"No, I don't think I do an awful lot for Peter in the hots department. I think he is more interested in a different kind of woman. Probably younger than me and perhaps a bit more petite."

Isabel did not seem affected by the self disparagement in this explanation and Dillon asked again.

"Do you think he has got a mistress?"

"Oh, yes very probably but I really don't care. If he dies, all of the house and the business will come to me. That would serve him and the little tart right."

"If indeed there is one." Dillon reminded her of the hypothetical nature of their discussion before continuing, "Do you want him to die?"

Neither the shocked denial nor the hesitation that Dillon would have expected in her response materialised. Instead she answered in slow deliberate tones.

"Yes, sometimes. Pretty often in fact." She even managed to smile as she replied and Dillon felt that he did not wish to pursue this line of thought any further.

There were two areas, however, in which Dillon made it clear that he had no desire to engage in conversation. These were his work and his views on the situation in Ulster. If these topics arose through some inadvertent trigger he would respond in the most perfunctory of forms.

Isabel soon learned the message behind his tone. They were sitting on his bed one Friday afternoon in September 1972. They had finished making love and Dillon had left to prepare two cups of coffee in the kitchen. It was only days after the gun battle at Furstenfeldbruk airport at which the police had shot dead five Arab terrorists who had been involved in holding Israeli athletes hostage at the Munich Olympic Games. They had talked about this event earlier on and Dillon had expressed the opinion that it was the correct tactics to deal with murderers. When he returned with the drinks, Isabel had switched on the radio and was listening to further reports and analyses of the incident. She was still astonished that Dillon should hold this view and had determined that she would again raise the subject.

"Remember you said earlier on that these terrorists got what they deserved?"

Dillon shifted restlessly on the bed and then moved to an armchair facing Isabel. He took a sip from his cup and laughed an uncomfortable laugh.

"You must think that's a bit like the pot calling the kettle black, and you're probably right. It's just that the madness over there sometimes affects your sense of reason."

His language sometimes puzzled her. He very rarely referred to Ulster by name. The terms 'over there', 'back home' or 'across the water' were generally the closest he came to geographical accuracy. Isabel wondered whether this was an opportunity to find out more about not only what Dillon really thought about the situation in Ulster but also about Dillon himself. She was prevented though from leading her next question by a knock at the door. Then Timms shouted, "John there's a phone call for you."

Neither Isabel nor Dillon had heard the phone

ring and Dillon very rarely received calls. Even though he noted the tone of urgency in his flatmate's voice he still felt a considerable sense of surprise and inconvenience.

"Is it possible for you to take a note of the number and I'll call back in half an hour or so?", he shouted to Timms through the door of his bedroom.

"John, I think you should take this call now, O.K.?"

Chapter 10

Dillon excused himself to Isabel and left the bedroom. He picked up the receiver and introduced himself to the caller.

"Hello, John Dillon here."

"John, it's Charlie McLean." Dillon stood bolt upright on this identification and some colour drained from his face.

"Commander, we don't often get calls at home from you. How can I help you?"

"I've got some terrible news for you John. Your brother was shot dead today. He was a brave man. He was killed carrying out some important work for us."

The pause lasted for a full thirty seconds before Dillon spoke again.

"Just a moment, Commander." He put the receiver down and went over to ensure that the door of the lounge was firmly closed. "Thank you for letting me know, Commander. Have you already let my father know?"

"Yes of course, John. Your father was the first to know. Even though he's retired from active service, he's still an important man in this outfit. It's likely to be in the mainland papers sometime over this weekend. I wanted to let you know beforehand."

"Does this compromise my security clearance to work over here?"

"No. I shouldn't think so. It just brings home the importance of developing that alias and new identity for you. But if you want to call it a day over there and come home we can arrange that for you John."

"No, I'll be coming across for the funeral, but I'm in the middle of a few projects here that I would want to finish."

"Good man, John. That's what Jimmy and your Dad would want. I'll have a word with you at the funeral. Gerry will make all the necessary travel arrangements for you."

Without a word Dillon brushed past Timms and returned to his bedroom. Isabel was still sitting on the bed finishing her coffee. Dillon looked at her and then deliberately sat on the armchair. She put the cup down and asked. "Is everything all right?"

An uncomfortable silence pervaded the room. Dillon realised that to share his news with her would jeopardise his own situation and yet he desperately wanted to be comforted. He thought nervously for an answer. "No, I'm afraid I've just had some bad news from home, but I don't want to talk about it and besides you wouldn't be able to understand. You are just too far removed from it all and I think it's better if it stays that way."

Isabel didn't understand him but she could see his lip trembling as he spoke. She stood up and pulled him over to her. They lay back on the bed and he buried his face in her chest. She was just able to just hear a very gentle sobbing. She stroked the back of his head and it occurred to her that in her hands she held a very vulnerable child. Her feelings for him changed in a way that was not only outwith her experience but also exceeded her abilities to comprehend. The change though was as all consuming as that metamorphosis that allows a caterpillar to come out of the cocoon as a butterfly.

The door opened suddenly and Timms enquired whether Dillon was alright. The object of his concern looked up and nodded, a gesture sufficient to allow Timms to withdraw. Isabel resented this intrusion. She felt that it was strange that in all the time she had been visiting the flat, Timms had been a paradigm of discretion but after the phone call he had burst into the room without warning. She continued to comfort Dillon and felt very protective towards him.

Dillon lay in Isobel's bosom for a full quarter of an hour and neither spoke a word. He then started to kiss her chest and she raised his head so that their lips could meet. He stroked her hair and kissed her eyelids. She held him tightly and whispered his name, but this time she called him 'John'. They kissed again and then Dillon helped Isabel to undress. She, in turn unbuttoned Dillon's shirt and released him from his trousers. They made love. This time it was a very gentle form of lovemaking and Isabel understood that they would not play the domination games again. When they had finished, they lay embracing each other. Isabel told Dillon that she would stay with him to morning if he wished.

"Wouldn't Peter want to know where you had been if you stay out all night?" asked Dillon in response to her offer.

"Oh, he might. And then again he might not be that interested. It doesn't really matter. It's you that it's important just now."

"No, go home Isabel. If we decide to confront Peter with our relationship then let's choose the moment to do so. I'm just not up to that right now. I get confused by the whole situation across the water. And I'm caught in the bloody middle of it all. It screws me up and it feels all the worse that I can't talk to you about it. Fucking, fucking madness."

This was the closest to an expression of his feelings about the work that he undertook that she had heard from Dillon. She asked gently, "Is it all madness? Surely there's a purpose to what you're doing? I remember your speech in the "Derry Bar". You made me feel that you understood precisely what was happening in Ireland."

"I will be the last person on earth to understand it. I just feel that I want to keep everyone away from it. Do you know your husband the other day mentioned to me the idea that he would come across the water to see with his own eyes where his money is going? Silly bugger.''

Isabel's eyes widened with interest. ''Why would he be silly to do that?''

''Come on Isabel. You're an intelligent woman, work it out for yourself.'' In spite of this invitation, however, Dillon continued to explain without permitting her time to respond. ''If he were to see any of our safe houses or see any of the field officers over there, he would have information that could do us a lot of harm.''

Isabel remained interested but she detected that Dillon not only considered that her questions were driven by a frivolous curiosity but also betrayed a basic naiveté in respect of the sort of activities in which he was engaged.

''So, just say for arguments sake that Peter did go over to see where the money was going; what would happen?''

''That's a non question: he wouldn't be allowed to see anything. Nobody would take him.''

She persisted, ''But if he was taken, what would they do to him.''

Dillon looked at her, in disbelief that she had had to ask the question. ''They'd kill him, of course.''

''What if he just stopped allowing the collections to be taken.''

''We couldn't allow that, the punters would hear about it and doubt our resolve or worse still another pub might learn about it and do the same. No, we would need to find an effective deterrent to stop that spreading.''

Isabel nodded her head. She was coming close to knowing all that she needed to know. She asked another question seeking both a confirmation of her assumption and a conclusion to her enquiry.

''So how exactly would you prevent that?''

''He'd probably receive the same treatment either way. We would kill him. It would just be a little harder to carry out. It's always easier if they come to our premises.''

Isabel was no longer shocked by her lover's sang froid. This was the answer that she had expected and she felt satisfied that with difficulty and persistence it was the one she had obtained. Isabel now prepared to leave.

After she had gone, Dillon came and joined Timms in the kitchen. Timms put his arm around his shoulder and said, ''John I'm really sorry about your brother. I only met him a couple of times but I heard a lot of good things about him.''

''Thanks, Gerry. I'll miss him.''

Then Timms started to speak in a more hesitant fashion. ''John, I know it's none of my business but you're seeing a lot of that Isabel Armstrong. It doesn't make our work any easier if you form attachments. Don't go and get too fond of her now.''

As soon as he said this Dillon turned round to

face him. "You're right, Gerry, it is none of your business. I've just lost a brother. I don't need a keeper."

"O.K. John, you know what you are doing."

The response this time was more conciliatory as Dillon sought to find a truce to their incipient altercation.

"Thanks, Gerry. I'm sorry. I didn't mean to jump down your throat. But there's nothing to worry about, she's just a bit of skirt, nothing else. Good in the sack, but nothing will come of it, I assure you, my friend. Celia is still too important to me."

This was the first occasion that Timms had heard his colleague mention his wife's name.

Chapter 11

The links between the situation in Northern Ireland and the King's Own Scottish Borderers can be found in the very inception of the regiment. In March 1689 the government of Britain was in a state of flux. The Prince of Orange, to become King William III, had arrived and taken the throne after the flight to France of his deposed father in law, King James. Not only in Ireland, however, was there resistance to this new Protestant king, but supporters of the Stewart dynasty engaged in rebellion in Britain itself.

In Edinburgh it took only two hours for the third Earl of Leven to raise a force, after the rumour was heard that the Jacobites intended to seize the town. The Edinburgh Regiment suffered a heavy defeat at Killiecrankie, but survived that and other battles to become the King's Own Scottish Borderers in 1805. Its soldiers still wear the Leslie tartan in commemoration of the family of the Earl of Leven who raised the regiment to protect the good citizens of Scotland's capital, frightened by a force that they believed would lead to an erosion of their religious rights and liberties.

It is essentially a regiment of the Scottish Borders and its recruitment is focused on this area. Consequently it is recognised as being very much a family regiment. The combinations and permutations of brothers, fathers and sons, uncles and nephews are all to be found amongst the ranks of this regiment.

Ian Maxwell had joined the regiment in the early 1960's to escape the large council housing estate of Lochside that sits on the north side of Dumfries. His friends had secured employment in either the plastics factory or the rubber works that dominate the economy of this area. Having spent his formative years in the shadow and residue of the second World War, he had decided at an early age that he wanted to be a soldier. Unlike so many children he had held on to this ambition and had presented himself at the recruiting office in the town the very day he left school.

He completed his training at the barracks in Berwick on Tweed and was posted to Germany, where he played his part in the cold war that was being enacted in that divided country. He then saw active service fighting the Arab tribesmen in Aden. Throughout all of this he rose through the ranks, becoming a non-commissioned officer and ending up as a sergeant. He was immensely proud of his three stripes. His other main source of professional pride came when his nephew and god-son, Paul Maxwell, announced at a family gathering, on one occasion that he was home on leave that he wished to follow in his uncle's footsteps and join the army. Although Paul was then too young to leave school, his uncle arranged for him to join the preparatory school, the Junior Leaders. His passing out parade to join the K.O.S.B. was watched by his mother and father with an ambivalence of pride and apprehension. Theirs was a justified concern. Less than a year later, Paul then 17½, was shot dead by a sniper's bullet as he patrolled the Bogside area of Londonderry.

The regiment had only been on this particular tour of Northern Ireland for six weeks but were already well known and generally disliked by the Catholic communities in Belfast and Londonderry. Within these enclaves the soldiers who wore the K.O.S.B. badge were referred to as the Kings Own Scottish Bastards.

It had been a quiet Saturday morning; Private Maxwell, as part of the six soldiers that made up number one patrol, was standing at an old stone arch that acts as an entrance to the walled city, assisting the R.U.C conduct personal searches of the shoppers as they passed through the gates. He was surprised at the resignation that the local population showed at being asked to open bags or occasionally being frisked. In rare instances someone would hurl abuse at either one of the soldiers or one of the policemen, but most had learned that to do so was tantamount to actually requesting a full body search. Consequently they passed on their way with a sullen silence or indifferent glances. Sometimes women would even sustain through the search the bland conversations in which they had been engaged before they were stopped, as though they were oblivious to the intrusion on their lives.

His corporal was sitting in a grey armoured vehicle a few yards away when he called the younger Maxwell and the other soldiers over. ''Seems like number three patrol has run into trouble with the locals down in Westland Street. We've to go down there and bail them out.''

Westland Street runs away from the city walls through the centre of the Bogside and was less than a quarter of a mile from where they were. Maxwell also knew that his uncle would be leading number three patrol. When they arrived the driver of the armoured car could see that a crowd of about fifty youths were hurling stones and bottles at a group of soldiers, perhaps a dozen or so crouched in three consecutive doorways. Occasionally one of the besieged party would fire off a plastic bullet when the crowd came too near. Sergeant Maxwell, a recognised marksman held a Self Loading Rifle in his hands. He was comforted to know that his bullets were not plastic, but like the rest of the soldiers serving in the Province, was under strict instructions only to fire live ammunition when directed by a superior officer or when he could clearly see that his target was in possession of a weapon. The armoured car did not slow down as it came through the Bogside and the crowd was scattered. It quickly regrouped and a hail of missiles was directed at the soldiers as they came out of their vehicle.

"The crowd's getting bigger every minute", said Maxwell to the newly arrived corporal.

"Well more of us and some R.U.C. boys will be here pretty soon. We were just up the hill when we got the call to act as the cavalry."

In fact another five minutes passed without any sign of rescue. Other forces had tried to enter the Bogside from the West End, but had met road blocks just after they passed Brooke Park Hospital and had been delayed. Radio contact assured Sergeant Maxwell that assistance would be directly on hand but the crowd's spirit of daring was increasing in direct proportion to its size. When the braver members of the baying mob were taking shelter behind the cars parked next to the armoured vehicle he decided that he had to charge. The helmets and visors would offer protection against the flying bricks and bottles that would greet them. Those soldiers with shields and truncheons would lead the charge, followed by those with the wide mouth ersatz shotguns that spat out the plastic bullets and finally Maxwell himself would bring up the rear prepared to discharge his weapon if any of those under his command got into trouble, in spite of what the current Queen's Regulations had to say on that practice.

The crowd dispersed as soon as the soldiers

charged. Two prisoners were taken and after receiving hefty clouts from the batons were thrown into the back of the armoured car. Private Paul Maxwell saw one youth who had been at the vanguard of the attacks on them disappear into a house in Butcher Street which adjoined Westland Street. He and another soldier followed him through the open door. Neither heard or heeded the Sergeant's shouts of rebuke. They came out of the rear of the house into a back green with their quarry nowhere to be seen. They were now in an enclosed space surrounded by the windows and rear entrances of all the other houses in the block. They realised together their mistake and turned to retrace their steps. Before he could cross the threshold to safety, Private Paul Maxwell heard a loud bang and felt a searing burning pain in his back. His uncle reached him a matter of seconds later, but he was already dead.

Sergeant Maxwell returned to Dumfries for his nephew's funeral but was back on duty less than a week later. The Friday morning after his compassionate leave was over he was involved in helping the R.U.C. conduct a security check by setting up a roadblock just on the Belfast side of Balygawley. The army, initiating a new strategy in their fight against terrorism, had deployed a number of powerful directional microphones which were hidden at the roadside. The traffic would build up until the queue stretched for about a hundred yards, then an R.U.C.

officer would ask the motorists to wind down their windows and turn off the engines. Once the noise of the running engines abated, the soldier sitting in the small makeshift hut at the side of the roadblock could clearly hear the conversations of the unsuspecting and frustrated motorists. This tactic had revealed a prolific amount of information about the motorists' personal lives and their feelings towards the security forces. It was about to prove its worth, now, with a far more significant revelation.

James Stewart and Bob McConachie were returning from Enniskillen where they had bought a number of guns from a rather unscrupulous farmer from Sligo. Stewart was driving and was the first to notice the block.

"Oh fuck, this is what we don't need."

"Don't worry, Jim. It's only a routine stop. We'll be on our way in a minute."

The policeman politely asked Stewart to stop running the engine and assured both men that the delay would be kept to an absolute minimum. Stewart grew anxious and enquired of his companion as to whether the cache would escape discovery if there was a search of the car. Sixty yards down the road in the hut a corporal with headphones over his ears beckoned Lieutenant Pound over.

"Listen to this will you, sir?"

A tape was replayed and Stewart's strong Ulster tones could be heard instigating the dialogue with a question to his companion.

"Are you sure the pieces are under the carpet."

"Of course they fuckin' are. Now just stop worrying will you. The peelers can smell fear ye know."

"Right", said Pound "that's good enough for me. Let's tear that car apart. Where's it located corporal?"

"Around mike 3, lieutenant. I reckon given the clarity of the sound, it must be right across from it. I can only hear two men talking, so that's what you are looking for."

Pound went out of the hut, signalled Maxwell and two other soldiers to come with him and proceeded to the spot where he knew that microphone 3 was hidden. An R.U.C. sergeant was standing close by and Pound approached him to share his suspicions. Stewart could not help notice the two men constantly cast glances in his direction. When their car seemed to be singled out for the attention of the R.U.C. Sergeant a cold sweat broke out on Stewart's brow. The Sergeant indicated that he wished the window to be rolled down yet again. It was explained that on the basis of new information that it had been decided to make a more thorough search of this vehicle. The passenger started to object but his protestations were peremptorily dismissed. It had been left to Stewart alone to take the only action that would save him from arrest. He opened the driver's door with a sudden explosion of force. It banged into the policeman's groin and sent him reeling away from the car. The attacker was propelled out by the coil of fear and had sprinted to the fence at the other side of the road before the shouts demanding him to stop were uttered. Stewart ignored them, vaulted the fence and continued to exhort his limbs to carry him away. All sounds were blanked out from his mind, save for the noise of his painful breathing, struggling against his own exertions for the lungfuls of air that he required to make good his escape.

On the other side of the car Lieutenant Pound shouted to Maxwell, "You're a marksman, sergeant?"

"I am, sir."

"OK. on you go man. Bring the bastard down. Shoot to the legs only though. I want to talk to him."

As Maxwell marched across the road the tears that he had held within him at his nephew's funeral now struggled for their release. They bit into his eyes and he wiped them aside. When he lay down on the grassy verge at the side of the road, he pointed his rifle at the target now almost half way across the field. The sights focused on the largest single area, the upper body and the trigger was squeezed, until it proffered no more resistance. The recoil from the gun banged against the sergeant's shoulder and he let out the breath that he had been holding. By the time he had started to rise to his feet, Pound, the R.U.C. sergeant and a handful of other soldiers had passed over him and were running to the spot where Stewart's body now lay motionless on a little mound of stained grass.

He picked up the rifle and slowly followed them. He, alone at that moment, knew what they would find. It is said that with the most favourable angle of descent, the standard issue S.L.R can propel a bullet for almost a mile. At fifty yards it hits its target with a frightening force. The party could see at the epicentre of the purplish stain on the back, the wound where the bullet had entered. When the body was turned over another larger bloody hole was spread over the chest of the corpse. Pound gazed for a moment into the distance. He wondered where the missile had finally embedded itself. It seemed, like the moving finger, it had done its work and carried on.

"I told you the bloody legs, sergeant. Call yourself a marksman?"

The lieutenant's face was puce with anger as he berated Maxwell when the sergeant finally forced his way into the small semi-circle that hovered around the body.

"I'm sorry sir. They did'nae teach me to shoot legs in Aden. Maybe something to do with the enemy we were fighting at that time being a bunch of dirty wogs, eh sir? As opposed to this lot sir, white men and all that. Anyway we still have a live one back at the car. We can kick the shit out of him while we question him about his pal, here.''

''You are on a charge, Sergeant.''

''Yes sir. At least I'm fuckin' alive, sir.''

It is an essential part of the human condition that death impacts upon survivors. The end of one human life has repercussions on the lives of others in the same way that a brick thrown into a pond will create a series of concentric ripples each one a little further away from the point of impact until the force is eventually extinguished. The deaths of James Stewart and Private Paul Maxwell would not provide exceptions to this rule.

Chapter 12

In a flat in the predominantly middle class area of Malone Road, Belfast, Commander Charles McLean held the phone tightly against his ear in a room that had been furnished to serve as an office. It resembled other offices in many respects. It had two desks each holding a telephone and various pieces of paper. Unlike most other offices, however, loaded revolvers were kept in the drawers of the desks and the door was always locked and bolted. On one of the walls a large flag was pinned up. It was almost a Union Jack but at its centre there was a red hand on a star shaped white background. Around the top of this motif, the words 'Ulster Freedom Fighters' had been emblazoned, whilst underneath it, was sown the maxim, 'What We Have, We Hold'.

Charles McLean sat behind the desk nearer the window on a seat that revolved in such a way that let him digress from studying the papers on his desk, to watching the world go by, without having to stand up. At the other desk which was beside the door and in front of a fixed chair, his assistant, David Norris, busied himself.

McLean, even though he was the senior officer, always had a great need to tell Norris precisely what he was doing. He put the phone down and waited for his assistant to raise his head.

"Poor bugger. First his wife shot by those

murdering Republican bastards and now his brother done in by the British army. He really has got caught in the crossfire. It was his twin brother you know."

Norris did know both that the person at the other end of the phone line to whom the Commander was now referring was Dillon and that Jim Stewart was Dillon's twin brother."

"They're Dick Stewart's boys aren't they?" It was common knowledge within the organisation that they were but Norris had detected that his boss wanted to talk and this question provided a good opening.

"Yes, they are. Good boys both of them, but old Dick has been one of us since he was a boy, so you would expect nothing less. I remember when he married that Taig. Wouldn't listen to us, and could only attend the meetings when she didn't know. I remember she threatened to report him and all of his friends to what she called "the authorities" unless he left the organisation. She eventually ran away from him and sent the boys to a Catholic school. Can you imagine that, being sent to a Catholic school for the first time when you're thirteen? Oh, they got bullied something awful by the priests, the teachers and the other boys. Then they refused to go to Mass and Confessions. There must have been terrrible rows in that house before their Dad nabbed them one day."

"Did their mother ever try to get them back?"

"She threatened to go to Court, to the police,

the lot. But she was staying with her folks at the time, so we had a word with the kids' grandad and explained that if she were inclined to talk about the things she had heard or tried to snatch them back it would be worse for all of them.''

"So they lived with their Dad. Up in Antrim, wasn't it?"

"Aye, just outside Cushendall. Deep in the Glens, hidden from the troubles. Now we've lost Jim. He'll be missed. He was a good soldier." Mclean sighed and returned to looking out of the window. He had had enough of discussion with Norris for the time being.

Jim Stewart's body was released to his family six days after the shooting. They had been advised of this time scale and had arranged for the funeral on that same day. It was to be a big occasion. McLean had described the forthcoming funeral in a speech the previous evening as an opportunity not just to grieve for the loss of a friend so cruelly taken, but also an opportunity to celebrate that soldier's many victories in the fight for his country. Timms had made the necessary arrangements for himself and Dillon to fly over that day.

They were met at Aldergrove Airport by a family friend and driven the short distance to Dick Stewart's house which was now on the outskirts of the county town of Antrim. As soon as they had cleared the airport security Dillon had announced that he could now formally resume his true identity and be referred to as John Stewart. Timms also announced his intention to introduce himself by his original name of Marshall, during their visit. Their driver craned his neck to look at the two passengers in the rear seat and remarked, "Well whichever one of the four the two of you are, it's good to have youse back."

When they arrived at the house Dillon was hugged by his father and it was a few minutes before he could ask the question which had occupied his thought for most of the fifty minute flight.

"Is my mother coming today?"

His father shook his head and explained that she had been informed that she would be welcomed but had already let them know that she chose to stay away.

After the burial, the mourners returned to a hotel that overlooked the shores of Lough Neagh. Dillon was kept busy receiving the condolences of various relatives. Later on, he noticed his father deep in discussion with McLean. Finally he was summoned across to join them and his father remarked, "I hear from the Commander here that you are in tow with a woman in Glasgow. Is it something your old Dad should know about?"

Dillon had expected to have received some tribute to his brother from McLean and was momentarily stunned by the question. He looked around to see if he could see Timms.

"I wonder who told the Commander."

McLean interrupted him to explain, "Gerry was only worried about your safety, John. He tells me this has been going on for a number of years. Is it serious? If so we can bring you and her back to Belfast. There's plenty of work here that doesn't require so much subterfuge, you know. I mean I imagine it must be a problem just keeping up the alias all the time. And what can you say when your young lady asks what you do for a living?"

Dillon laughed at the ideas of Isabel finding out what he did and the prospect of her returning to Belfast with him, but it was not a laugh that he shared. Instead he replied, "No, it's not serious at all Commander. She's just a friend."

His father remained curious, "You'll at least tell us her name"

"Isabel, Isabel Armstrong, Dad. I met her at a dance hall in Glasgow. The Plaza. I'll take you the next time you get across, Dad and see if we can fix you up too."

Dick Stewart mulled over the name, "Armstrong, eh? That sounds a good Protestant name, but you can't be too sure. Did you find out what school she went to?"

This time Dillon did not feel like laughing, but adjudged that tactic as being the quickest way of concluding the conversation. As he turned to leave them he said, "Don't worry, she's one of us alright."

Dick Stewart and McLean remained together. When Dillon was out of earshot McLean said, "He'll be O.K. He's done his stint in Glasgow though. I think taking everything into account a transfer may not be a bad idea. We need to develop the operation in Boston. Great city Boston. The most British of all American cities, you know. As you fly in you see all these pretty little houses with neat gardens. Sure for all the world it could be Ballymena or Bangor. I think your man there could be the very person to liberate a few greenbacks for the cause."

Dick Stewart nodded his agreement to this idea and added. "It's been a few years since my daughter in law was killed. Perhaps if this transfer was sooner rather than later it would just make sure that he doesn't get inveigled with someone we don't know."

"I need to clear it higher up the line and I need to arrange proper cover for him, but I think I can promise you that within, say, three months from now, the boy will be landing at Logan International."

Chapter 13

On the Sunday preceding the funeral, Peter Sullivan had wakened just in time to experience the last few moments of the forenoon. He had stayed in the pub well after closing time, imbibing with a few customers who had been invited to remain. Unfortunately for them the police decided, that night, to ensure that the licensing regulations were being fastidiously implemented in the "Derry Bar". The knock on the door and the light of the torch through the key hole warned Peter to the impending inspection. The drill of ushering the customers down to the cellar and impressing upon them the need for silence had been practised before. It was carried out with efficiency and the two policemen were then allowed entry. The drink offered to the constables was accepted as usual. As Peter was holding the door open for their departure, one of them remarked that a Chief Inspector had come down to observe the night shift at the station. It was possible that later on he might tour the area by car, stopping at any hostelry that still displayed lights or other signs of continued merry making. In view of this the constable suggested that when the after hours drinking corps arose from the cellar it would be prudent to truncate this session.

One of the women who had been drinking earlier in the evening in the company of some more regular customers proffered a solution to the assembled company. She suggested that they return to her home where they could continue their banter and drinking in a less anxious ambience. This new voice had frequented the pub on a number of previous occasions, but Peter had paid her scant regard and had only a vague notion from a distant discussion that her name was Ann.

The invitation had been made generally to those huddled around the bar. Sullivan was, though, astute and at that point sober enough to realise by the way she looked deliberately at him and smiled when it was issued that he would be particularly welcomed. He had seen that sort of look before. Ostensibly it conveyed friendship and warmth but in reality it told of desire. He studied closely his predator and wondered why he had not paid her greater attention earlier in the evening. She was much younger than him, somewhere in her very early twenties. She was dressed in a tight sweater and mini skirt, both of which flattered her figure. She wore heavy make up around her eyes and on her lips which added to her seductive appearance. Peter found the receipt of her favouritism to be flattering and was excited by the prospect of pursuing his interest. He decided that it would be churlish not to accept the invitation. The other customers also were aware that although they had been included, it was with somewhat less enthusiasm that she awaited their response. Even the other two women who had accompanied Ann that evening found that they had reason to decline the offer of further drink. Sullivan picked up a bottle of spirits as he left the bar and found himself alone with Ann in a taxi cab that sped towards Bridgeton Cross.

As they got out of the taxi she gripped his arm and asked him to be quiet as they went into the flat.

"How? Is your man sleeping?" enquired Peter.

"Naw, but the weans are."

"So what ages are they?"

"Seven and nine."

Peter's new found friend hardly seemed old enough to have children of that age, but another thought concerned him.

"So who is looking after them, the night?"

"I telt you, they're asleep. They don't need anyone to look after them and a girl's got to get out to enjoy hersel' once and a while, hasn't she?"

He would have started to question Ann on the ethics and risks of leaving them unattended in the house, had he felt more comfortable. Instead he decided to let the matter rest. She in turn poured large drinks from Sullivan's bottle, put a long playing record on the turn-table of the music centre and swayed provocatively in time to the music. Sullivan took off his jacket and moved across the room to be beside her. He tentatively put his arms around her waist. She moved into him and they started to kiss. As their mouths were locked together, her fingers played with the hair on the back of his head. She ensured that not the thinnest piece of paper could be slipped between them and could feel the surges of excitement heave within him as her body rippled over his front. When the song had finished she said, "It's late. Let's go to bed."

They finished making love and Sullivan lay beside her for a few minutes, thinking to himself. He felt no guilt or remorse, but rather a sense of pride. He had attracted and had bedded a beautiful woman almost half his age. It had been Isabel's decision to break off sexual relations but yet she continued to live in the house that he had obtained and to enjoy the profit that his business made. These actions, he told himself, vindicated this affair. She could not exploit him with impunity. He rose and started to get dressed. Ann turned round to look at him and asked, "Don't you want to stay till morning? You can sleep, now. I won't ask anything more of you till then."

This proposal was not without attraction, particularly when contrasted with the alternative of wandering around the empty, threatening streets of the Gallowgate at two o'clock in the morning looking for a vacant taxi. He thought, however of the two children and the prospect of hearing his presence explained to them.

He finished his dressing and replied, "Some other time, eh? I've got to go home now."

Ann added her own explanation, "Otherwise

you will get into trouble from the wife.''

"That's not what I was thinking about. It really doesn't matter whether my wife knows where I spent the night or not", he said truthfully before he left.

When he came downstairs to prepare breakfast for himself, Isabel had just returned from Mass and was making herself a cup of coffee. She offered him one and he nodded acceptance before sitting at the kitchen table.

She joined him and said, "You were late in last night."

"Was I?" He retorted using abruptness to cover his feelings of defensiveness.

"Just an observation. Let's try to remain civil to each other whilst we're living under the same roof."

"What do you mean 'whilst'. How's it going to change."

Isabel gave him the look that she used to use when she teased him.

"Oh, you might die tomorrow and I could inherit the lot."

Sullivan decided to avoid moving into a full blown argument and treat this remark as a joke.

"Not me, I'm a picture of health. Although I have to admit to having a bit of a headache this morning. The reason I was so late in was because a few of the regulars wanted to stay on for an after hours drink and I thought that to be the hospitable, affable landlord that I am, I should join them. It bloody hurts now though.''

Isabel doubted whether they had been drinking to half past two, but she had another matter of greater import that she wished to raise.

"Does that Mr Dillon still come and take protection money for looking after our pub."

Peter noticed the emphasis on the word 'our', but ignored it to address the question.

"It's not protection money but as a matter of fact, he does. Funny you should mention it now, I got a phone call from him yesterday to say that he couldn't come next Friday and would collect the money the week after. Something about a family funeral. I hope the lot of them have been struck down by a plague or something. Why are you asking that, just now?"

"I was just thinking of that first night that he came. You didn't even know whether the collection was for the Officials or the Provos. Have you found out yet?"

"I'm not that interested. I just pay up my contribution and hope he doesn't hang about."

Isabel stared at him and Peter realised his mistake.

"What? You mean it's not just a collection, that we are paying money as well. I'd bloody well call that extortion and what a fool you are if you don't know where the money is going. The guy could be conning you all this time. It might not even be going to Ireland, it could be going into his pocket. That would be a nice little racket, wouldn't it? And at our expense too."

This thought had in fact crossed Sullivan's mind before and he had raised it with Dillon. He felt that he had just about enough ammunition to defend himself.

"I thought about that, so one day I pulled Dillon over and said that I needed some proof as to where the money was going. I was even prepared to go across the water with him, but he said it wouldn't be safe or practical."

"So you just left it at that did you?"

Peter remembered wondering how sober he had been when he had voiced that suggestion. A wave of relief had swept over him when Dillon raised his objections and proffered other recourses. It did not seem necessary though to recount these particular thoughts to Isabel.

"No of course I didn't. I told him that if he couldn't give me satisfactory proof then the money would stop. So he showed me a letter signed by the Chief of Staff authorising him to collect money on behalf of the Provisional I.R.A. Some guy called Goulding, or something. Cathal Goulding, that's it. With a name like that you would have to be the big boss in the I.R.A., wouldn't you? It was on headed note paper as well."

The attempt to inject humour was ignored and

the derision in Isabel's voice was overwhelming, "So you're happy with that. You know who the Chief of Staff is and what his signature looks like, do you? It's probably on all their recruiting posters. God, you're an even bigger fool than I imagined."

"Isabel would you shut up for a minute and let me finish. Of course I realised that the letter could be a forgery and I told him so. He agreed to give me a Belfast telephone number to check him out. So I phoned this number and a woman answers. I told her who I was and that John Dillon had given me the number. It was all very organised, she said that she knew about the "Derry Bar" and that she would phone me back to confirm. Two minutes later the phone rings and this female voice tells me that I have got through to the headquarters of the Provisional I.R.A. I had the proof I was looking for. See, she couldn't say anything more because the line was probably bugged. So I think the guy's genuine, but if you really want to know the truth Isabel, I'm not that sure that I would mind if he wasn't. As long as the pub keeps making money and there's no more trouble, does anything else really matter?"

"Have you lost all your pride? Of course it matters if someone is taking a rise out of you and conning you out of money. What if folk got to hear that you had been led down the garden path for year after year? What would they think of you? Your father would turn in his grave. I can just hear him now behind that great bar in the sky saying to his pals 'I was right about the boy. He is a fool. I should have given the business to his brother'.''

This allusion to his father annoyed Peter. He had plans to play golf later that day and wished to be finished with the conversation. He snapped at her, ''Shut up Isabel. I've told you that I've checked it out.''

''That telephone number could belong to his Auntie, for all you know, and she's having a laugh at your, no - our, expense. You're still a wee boy when it comes to dealing with people, Peter. Your Dad would never have been palmed off so easily.''

''So what do you suggest that I do?''

''I think you got it right first time, yourself. You've got to go over there and see for yourself or else just stop paying the money.''

Peter had a very bad game of golf. His partner remarked that he seemed distracted.

Chapter 14

Dillon eventually came to the "Derry Bar", the Tuesday evening after the funeral. This period and the days on either side of it were traditionally the quietest times of the week in the pub. The weekend had passed and the money set aside for entertainment had been spent. On Thursday, the Corporation workers and those in a few other firms would be paid again and the cycle would start anew.

"I'm sorry about last week." Then almost as though he was remonstrating with himself for having made this apology, Dillon added. "As I said, though, I was called away to a family bereavement."

Sullivan poignantly didn't offer condolences or express any other form of sympathy. Instead he ushered Dillon to the furthest corner of the bar to say, "I've got to talk to you, John. Urgently."

"The last time you needed to talk to me urgently, someone had just tried to torch your pub. I thought that had stopped for good."

Peter became aware that a number of customers were looking intently in their direction and no doubt wondering why they had sought seclusion to conduct their discussion. When Peter had first rehearsed his strategy in his own mind for conducting this confrontation he had hoped that his adversary would indeed come at one of the quieter times of the week. He now realised that this had been a grave mistake. The lack of customers seemed to emphasise the clandestine nature of the little huddle in which the two men were immured. His discomfort was obvious. He shifted from foot to foot as he said, "Look, I can't talk here. Can I meet you tomorrow, outside the pub, somewhere?"

Dillon nodded his head, "Sure, Peter. No problem. We can have a drink in the town if you like. Lunchtime would be best, you say the place."

Peter knew the owner of the "Red Parrot" pub at the top of Buchanan Street. He could phone him and request the use of the office at the back of the premises for a brief meeting. The two men were coldly formal as they arranged a mutually convenient time. Dillon wrote it down in a pocket diary before receiving directions as how to reach the place. When the details were concluded he put the book away but in spite of the landlord's belief and fervent hope that their business had been postponed, he still remained standing, expectantly. Peter looked quizzically at him for a clue and when he failed to pick up any, his stomach began to churn. Eventually convinced by Peter's ashen appearance, that checkmate would shortly surely follow, Dillon smiled before he delivered what he believed to be the coup de grace of the first game of the evening.

"Isn't there something else you have for me? Like last week's collection. And I'm afraid that the one before that was not so good, so I am looking for a hundred and twenty five from you as well.

"You haven't understood John. That's what I want to talk to you about. I'm not going to give you another penny until I know where it's going."

Dillon's face reddened; he had underestimated his opponent's determination and resources in this psychological tussle. He was battling to control an anger inside of him. The funeral and the intervening period had afforded him an opportunity to think about the struggle in which he and his family were caught up and his resolve had hardened. The threshold of his tolerance towards those who did not understand had been crossed. With both hands he grabbed Peter by the lapels and pulled him over the bar until the space between their faces was no more than a couple of inches. He then said quietly, "It's you that doesn't understand. It's an irrevocable decision to fund the cause. You can't just pull out, like that. It's non-negotiable. Got it?"

Both men became aware that the whole of the bar had suspended their own discussions to give their full attention to this interaction. Dillon released his grip and started to smooth out Peter's jacket.

"I'm sorry Peter. That was not like me at all. I must be still upset about that funeral. I'm really sorry."

Peter had never seen Dillon being so profusely apologetic and it contrasted sharply with the image he held of him in his mind. He wouldn't let this confusion stand in the way of the point he wanted to make. He said in a voice just loud enough to allow the nearest of the customers who had been witness to his assault to hear.

"If you ever touch me again, I'll give you the biggest kicking you've ever had in your life."

"O.K. I've said I'm sorry but I do need the money now."

The note in Dillon's voice was not just apologetic or conciliatory. He almost seemed to be pleading now. The wolf had lain down and offered his throat. Peter had fully regained his composure and in spite, or perhaps because of Dillon's expression of aggression, felt more in control of the situation.

"The money's here but I told you if you want it you are going to have to talk seriously to me. No more palming me off with letters or phone numbers. I want to talk to the organ grinder not the monkey."

Dillon decided not to share the observation that this last remark had not provoked an immediate violent response only by an unusual effort of self restraint. The smile on his lips, however, was placed there by thoughts of self congratulation.

"Can you come with me just now then and we'll see if we can work something out?"

"Where do you want to go?"

"Let me take you to the dogs. Five past eight. We'll catch the second race if we leave now."

It took them only five minutes to drive to Shawfield Stadium and park. Dillon paid them both inside and passed a programme to Peter. This park had originally been constructed as a football stadium but served its new function well with the field enclosed by the racing track. They passed through a tunnel and emerged on the other side in the middle of the main concrete terrace. From here they could watch in the illumination of the giant floodlights, the crowd rushing to the bookmakers' stalls to place their bets and then back to the little huddles that congregated at strategic vantage points all around the stadium. The tannoy announced the crucial stages in the run up to the second race of the evening's meeting. The greyness of the weather seemed reflected in the shabbiness of the clothes of those engaged in this frenetic activity. The faces as they studiously poured over the programme and the forms of the canine athletes, were so intent as to be almost expressionless. When they rose from their papers and talked to one another they became animated but it was a form that seemed to tell Peter more about a concern with losing than enjoyment. As the countdown proceeded, the two men ascended the stairs of the terracing by squeezing through the mass of bodies. In front and above them Peter noticed a large corpulent man wearing a camel overcoat and gold rings on each of his fingers. This display of opulence set him apart from the rest of the crowd. He smiled at Peter's companion and the same glistening metal was visible in his mouth. Peter saw him approach and thought that he would embrace Dillon but his lips changed direction at the last moment to allow him to whisper into Dillon's ear. Then he scurried away into the darkness. Dillon looked pleased with himself again.

"Do you fancy a flutter, Peter? Number two dog is worth a couple of quid in this race."

"Are you putting a bet on?"

"Not in this race. I've got a fancy in the fifth, though. I was going to come along here after I'd been to the "Derry Bar", anyway."

"I'll leave it as well just now."

Peter was busy watching the white coated handlers load the dogs into the traps and didn't see Dillon's lips mouth, "You've already gambled enough."

The 'rabbit' passed the traps and triggered their opening. Thirty five seconds later the race was over. The favourite, the dog with a large number two emblazoned on the coat on its back, had won easily.

"Well I should have taken your advice." Peter said to Dillon.

"You always should", retorted Dillon. He put his arm on Peter's shoulder and turned him around, so that he was facing the entrance to a tunnel.

"I'm a member of the club here. If we go upstairs, we can get a drink and find somewhere to chat in relative privacy." As they went through the tunnel and climbed a flight of stairs, Dillon explained that it was in this very stadium that he had first heard of the "Derry Bar" and of Peter expressing his sympathies for the Republican cause. Peter could not guess which of his customers would have imparted this information so freely but knew that he had no reason to thank him. Most of the other patrons of the club sat at the seats beside the windows in order that they could follow the dog racing. Consequently the area in front of the bar was almost deserted. They found a table in a corner and Dillon summoned a waitress by smiling at her. He addressed her by name and ordered a soft drink for himself and invited Peter 'to have something a little stronger to calm his nerves'.

"I don't need to have my nerves steadied. It's you that's got everything to lose".

Dillon did not reply. He merely stared at him; a cold, threatening stare. Then he noticed the waitress looking at him impatiently. Whatever was going on between these two gentlemen was of no concern to her. The delay in placing their order did however inconvenience her.

"Do ye want a drink, or no?", she asked.

"A pint of lager", answered Peter without any courtesy.

They remained silent until the drinks were brought. Then Dillon moved his seat just a little closer to Peter and said, "Right Peter, What's bothering you?"

Peter recalled that it was less than half an hour ago that he had been man-handled by Dillon when he previously tried to declare his current stance. His reply, consequently, was without warmth and sought to negate the intimacy that Dillon had attempted to inject into their discussion.

"I've told you what's bothering me. I don't really know where all this money I'm giving you every fortnight is going. It's a fair amount and for all I know it could be going straight into your pocket. I think I'm entitled to a bit of proof. I mean what if a customer asks me how I know that you're pukka. I'd look a right fool if all I can tell them is that I've seen a letter and got a phone number. I need something else to convince them that I'm not being done." Peter was thoughtful for a moment and then corrected himself, "I mean, that they, the punters, are not being conned when they give to the collections."

His companion stroked his chin and continued to look intently at him as he responded, "O.K Peter. I can appreciate that, but what proof can I give you? We're not like the Red Cross you know. It's a bit more difficult to supply you with testimonials of our work or to give you the address of our offices."

"No, but you can take me over there and introduce me to some of your associates and then if any of the punters were to ask I could say that I've seen things with my own eyes."

Dillon shook his head. He understood now that this request was about Peter establishing kudos for himself. He remembered the time that Peter had recalled to Isabel his bravery in dealing with those thugs that had invaded his bar that eventful Saturday afternoon.

Peter was thinking about Ann.

"Look, if it's about establishing your credentials, why don't we disappear and then say that you've been staying with me in a flat in the Falls Road. We could piss off to London for a couple of days and then return with a few good stories."

That idea was initially not without attraction. It would certainly meet the demands from Ann. Then Peter remembered Isabel's portrayal of his father's assessment of the steps he had taken to guard against being duped. He felt that he was now being presented with a real opportunity to display his mastery over his opponent. His father would be proud if he was looking down. Dillon's willingness to collude in a fictitious trip could only indicate the strength of his own negotiating position. In spite of the voices that he had previously recognised as common sense and self preservation screaming inside his head, he took immense pleasure trumping Dillon's last card.

"You've got the wrong man. I'm here tonight not to get good stories to tell in the pub. I've been talking about preserving my reputation in business. I'm not kidding. I really do want tangible proof that you are who you say you are. Otherwise no more money and no more collections in the ''Derry Bar''. He tried hard to use a tone of voice that suggested tenacity.

''Peter, I have to tell you that what you are suggesting is very dangerous. It might not seem a big thing to you going across the water, to meet a few folk, but there's a completely different set of rules over there. People would get nervous if they thought you knew who they were or where they could be found. Publicity is the last thing my colleagues want.''

''I've been a good friend to your organisation for three years now. Surely they would recognise that. They should also know that I can keep my mouth closed.'' Dillon was about to argue with him over this last point, but Peter still imbued with a sense of holding the advantage in this discussion cut him off abruptly, ''I've told you, John, I need that tangible proof. That's not negotiable. Now if you don't have the authority to arrange it then you had better speak to someone higher up who can. And once I've met some of the people involved in the operational side of things, then you can have your money.''

Dillon realised that to continue to spell out the dangers to Peter would only take them deeper and deeper into the impasse. He conceded, ''O.K.

Peter, I'm not going to guarantee anything for I suspect the answer will be 'no', but if you really want me to have a word with somebody higher up the tree than me, then that's precisely what I'll do.''

The public address system truncated Peter's gloating by announcing the dogs for the fifth race. The two men left the club bar and returned to the terracing. A large shed had been set aside to allow the bookmakers to use upturned wooden boxes as small platforms from which they might conduct their business. The boards that stood on these benches displayed their names and underneath was chalked the various betting odds for each dog.

"Watch the odds on dog number one", advised Dillon.

The first showing put it at 5 to 2. It went suddenly to 3 to 1 and then 4 to 1. Dillon grabbed Peter's sleeve and shouted 'now' into his ear before leaving him to approach the small dais nearest them. Peter heard him place his bet '£500 top dog.' He repeated this at the next two bookmaker's stalls before the odds fell as dramatically as they had increased. Peter had followed the lead and had managed to give the two ten pound notes that his wallet contained and the same instruction to the first bookmaker before the odds were changed. They ran to the waist high wall over which they could follow the progress of their selection. It started in the inside trap and was trailing the rest until the pack came to the last bend of the race. Then dog number one seemed to develop wings that allowed it to go past all of its rivals in the blinking of an eye and finish in first place. Peter had the grace to congratulate Dillon. He had won the argument of the night, he could not begrudge Dillon winning his wager, particularly when Dillon had allowed him to share in his good fortune. Peter collected his stake and winnings but noticed the far more substantial amount being gathered in Dillon's hands. The thought that Dillon had a secret as potentially valuable as the alchemist's formula for turning base metal into gold prevented Peter from restricting his curiosity. He asked, "How did you know that was the bet of the whole meeting? How did you know it was going to win?"

"I didn't. I just knew the other four were going to lose. I've already told you about my organisation's power of persuasion."

As soon as he said this, he regretted disclosing his method to Peter. He avoided further questions by noting, "Turn up for the books that, eh? I come to collect money off you and you not only refuse to give it to me but you make a tidy little profit as well."

Dillon then said he was going to leave as he had other business to which he must attend that evening and offered Peter a lift back to the "Derry Bar". Peter declined so Dillon told him that he would contact him in the next few days to communicate his superior's thoughts on the request for a visit. After allowing sufficient time to pass to ensure that he would not be seen going through the car park by Dillon, Peter left the stadium as well. He hailed a taxi and gave the driver Ann's address. He wondered how he might direct the discussion to present himself with an opportunity to tell her that he would be going to Belfast in the very near future.

Chapter 15.

There was a widespread fear in Dillon's organisation that both incoming and outgoing phone calls could be tapped by the security forces. Consequently an elaborate precautionary system had been devised. This meant that each month Dillon received through the post a letter that contained only a Belfast telephone number written on a single sheet of paper. He used this constantly changing number to contact McLean to report on the progress of his operations or to receive further instructions. This would be done in one of two ways; either he could phone the number at a specific time each week when he knew that McLean would make himself available or if the matter was of greater urgency he could phone and request that he speak to the Commander. The latter case necessitated him phoning back in an hour, when McLean would have been contacted and made his way to the safe number. In either event the calls were always made from a different public telephone kiosk on each occasion.

Dillon did not think that Peter's ultimatum deserved any greater priority than being placed on the top of the agenda for the routine telephone discussion scheduled for the afternoon of the following day. McLean listened carefully as Dillon recalled his efforts to persuade Peter to pay up. He asked questions to confirm his understanding of what Dillon described as an impasse.

"So, he knows that he could be in danger if he continues to insist on coming over here, does he?"

"Well I've spelled it out as clearly as I can, but the man's a fool. I don't think he really has a clue what he would be letting himself in for. He's adamant though, he won't give me a penny or even let the collections take place unless he sees for himself."

"Sees what?", said McLean who was struggling to learn exactly what Peter was seeking.

"I don't think he really knows himself. He seems to have an idea that we'll show him around and then he can go back and tell all his pals about the trip. I think he wants to play the big man."

"So what do you suggest, John.?"

"I think we give him a right fright and if he continues not to pay, a bit of lead at the back of his head would act as a deterrent to anybody else with the same idea about resigning."

"John, you're a good man but you don't think past the end of your nose. If we duffed him up or even put a bullet in him others might start to think that we are just a bunch of hoodlums. Maybe, they would start asking questions as well. It's important that we keep the money rolling in. That's as good a weapon as the guns and bullets it buys. If Mr Sullivan wishes to come across and meet us to talk about continuing the collections and donations then that's precisely what we'll arrange. Phone me again at this number at seven-thirty tonight and I'll tell you the arrangements for the trip.''

Dillon's surprise at this response changed to anger as he made his way back to the flat. All his instincts warned him against letting outsiders meet anybody they didn't have to meet or know anything they didn't require to know. He was also aware that he would have to admit to Dillon that he had erroneously anticipated his superior's response.

''Bloody fool'', he said to Timms when he found him in the kitchen, reading the newspaper beside a pile of unwashed crockery.

''What's that?'' exclaimed his startled colleague.

Dillon explained by telling him about the content of his telephone conversation. He concluded, ''I mean I thought we were supposed to work on a strictly need to know basis. Even if the bastard is given the fright of his life over there, he's going to have information on me that could be pretty lethal in the wrong hands.''

''They wouldn't expose you to that sort of risk, John. I doubt very much whether Mr Sullivan will be making the return trip at all. Doing the business over there just gives us the opportunity of obtaining better publicity photos.''

His friend looked bemused at Timms choice of words. The invitation to expand was seized almost with glee. ''I think what is likely to happen is that

Sullivan will be taken for a little motor car ride to the factory out of the way of prying eyes. Maybe they will crush his balls and record the screams on tape. Then they will shoot him and take a photo of the body with one of the boys standing over it. Armalite in his hand and a black balaclava over his face. He'll be standing underneath a big Republican flag. Just imagine how convincing those images would be if somebody else were to tell either you or me that they're are not going to pay up any more. Tricks of a dirty trade.''

The portrait being painted held Dillon's attention. He knew that the 'factory' was a shed belonging to a sympathetic farmer that overlooked Strangford Lough in which his organisation had conducted a number of tortures on errant informers or petty criminals who had transgressed against the community it purported to represent. He admitted that it was a very plausible theory particularly when contrasted with his first interpretation. It certainly was far more in accord with the mental image he held about the way the Commander went about his business. He wondered whether his relationship with the prospective victim's wife had been the impediment to him recognising for himself what now seemed the obvious explanation. This scenario, he thought, would make the humble pie that he would be forced to consume in front of Peter so much more palatable. He thanked Timms. He even started to think about photos that could be taken before Sullivan's punishment and which later could be used in his efforts to deter others from following a similar course. Perhaps one of himself and Peter standing together on the walls of Londonderry looking down to the distinctly identified ''Bogside Inn''. Timms hoped he had made an accurate assessment of the Commander's intentions but struggling against his instincts, he kept his concerns tightly locked up in the vault of his doubt.

The phone rang in the ''Derry Bar'', later that same evening and the Belfast accent asked to speak to Mr Sullivan.

''My apologies, Peter. It seems you were right and I was wrong. The folk across the water would be delighted to meet you to thank you personally for all you have done for the cause.''

Dillon was sure he could detect a gloating in Peter's response.

''No problem, John. It's always worth checking it out with the top man. Now when do I go?''

''We go next Monday, if that's alright with you. I'll be taking you over. We'll probably come back on Tuesday evening. Can you get a couple of days away, without anybody knowing where you're going?''

''Sure, I'll tell the staff I'm going golfing for a couple of days. This place almost runs itself anyway.''

There was a momentary silence on the line and then Dillon said, "What about Isabel?"

"Would you prefer I didn't say anything to her as well."

Dillon answered in a summary fashion, "Yes."

The conversation then moved to a conclusion, with Dillon telling Peter that he would meet him at the Central Station on Monday at a particular time. Dillon side-stepped the question about it being quicker by plane by briefly explaining that it was necessary for him to alternate between ferry and aeroplane. That way, he continued, would mitigate against the chances of him being recognised as a frequent traveller. He also explained that going as foot passengers meant that they would not have a car whose number could be logged. Discussing these practicalities reminded Peter of the previous occasion that he had considered the idea and had peremptorily dismissed it as being foolhardy. This impression recurred in his mind. He felt, however, that Dillon would not be open to the notion of postponing the trip and cancellation would be tantamount to humiliation. A silent curse was directed at Isabel whom he now viewed as the architect of this expedition.

Before he rang off, Dillon said, "Everybody over there presumes that this week's collection will go ahead and that you will bring the money you owe us."

Peter confirmed this presumption and became

aware that the balance of power had shifted once again.

The following day another phone call asking for Peter Sullivan was received. When Peter picked up the phone, however, he heard only a click before a low whine was emitted from the line to indicate that there was nobody, any longer at the other end.
Dillon's car drew up the gravel path of the Sullivans' drive. It had been a number of years since he had last visited, but the house and garden were unchanged. When Isabel came to open the door it was apparent that she was startled by Dillon's presence. She looked for a moment at him and blinked almost as though she was checking that her eyes were not deceiving her. Then she said, ''What are you doing here? I told you that we have nosy neighbours. The Andersons over there will make a point of telling Peter about the strange man who came to my door in the middle of the morning.''

She nodded her head in the direction of the next house and then waved. Dillon turned around and over a common hedge saw an elderly couple, standing side by side inside a large bay window to witness his arrival. Isabel flauntingly put her arms around his neck and led him inside the house.

''May as well be killed for a sheep as a lamb. That will give them something to talk about.''

She shut the door with a kick and started to kiss Dillon. He struggled to break free, protesting,

"Isabel, not now. I've got to talk to you. It's important."

He told her that Peter had persisted in going to Ireland with him. It was not completely unexpected when she replied that her husband had woken her up the previous night on his return from the pub to impart that same information. Dillon continued to stress how dangerous it would be. He asked her if she still had an iota of influence over Peter to try to persuade him to rescind his ultimatum and cancel the visit. Her agreement in this endeavour was secured but she also remarked that she did not hold much hope of success.

"O.K. Isabel I had to ask and I felt that I had to give you as much notice as possible. I'm sorry for having turned up unannounced like this. I've got to go now but I'll meet you tomorrow as usual."

"Maybe after the Belfast trip, we'll be able to meet a bit more regularly than just once a week."

It was a half smile, that almost spoke of pain, which crossed his lips as he responded, "We'll see."

Isabel was too preoccupied with her own thoughts to hear the lack of enthusiasm in his voice. As she showed him out they both noticed the Andersons still standing by their window. Isabel returned their stare and then gave them another wave of recognition. After a moment, they withdrew complaining to each other about Isabel's lack of manners.

Peter arrived back from the pub just before eleven o'clock that evening and, following his routine, went into the drawing room to watch television. He did not expect Isabel to join him as she would usually have been upstairs at that hour preparing for bed. When she did he wondered with what revelation she was preparing to confront him. After a few moments of sitting in silence she said to him. "Since you told me last night about this trip, I've been thinking about it. Mr Dillon will certainly know now that you're the sort of man who can't be mucked about. I reckon your Dad will be proud of the way you have handled all this."

He found it strange that she should use the future tense rather than the past subjunctive. But also he could not recall the last time he had received a compliment from his wife. He was uncertain how he should accept it but Isabel solved the problem by leaving the room before he had a chance to reply.

A taxi had been ordered to take him to Central Station the following Monday morning but when it arrived Peter found that he was not quite ready. He then realised that he had not allowed sufficient time to permit the cab to negotiate the morning's busy traffic into the town centre. Consequently he was almost twenty minutes late when he ran towards Dillon. A ticket was pressed into his hand and his companion directed him towards a platform and a waiting train. They found vacant seats and placed their luggage in the racks above their heads but had not time to sit down before the train jolted forward.

"You cut that pretty fine," said Dillon tersely, "I thought you'd changed your mind at the last minute.

Peter looked at the truculent gaze of the man opposite him. He wondered whether it was precipitated by his tardiness or simply by the very fact that he had chosen to make this journey. At various times Peter tried to strike up amicable conversation but was rebuffed with perfunctory replies. Dillon had a newspaper that he unfolded and raised it to cover his face. He hoped that this might convey the notion that he was in no mood for exchanging pleasantries. Just over two hours into the journey the train halted. Peter looked out of the window and saw a station sign announce the unfamiliar name of 'Barrhill'.

"Barrhill", said Peter to the newspaper in front of him. No reply was forthcoming and he decided to be more direct. "Do you know, John, where we are? I've never heard of Barrhill."

Dillon looked over his paper. He was struggling within himself not to be rude to the condemned man but he also had no desire to talk to him in any greater detail than was necessary.

"It's the last station in Ayrshire. We'll be in Stranraer in a little over half an hour."

The newspaper was then raised again and Peter

understood that it was meant to serve as an obstacle to further discussion. The street sign reading 'Station Road' bears testament to the fact that at one time there was a train station in the town of Stranraer itself. Peter, however, found himself going through a long tunnel just after he had seen the first houses on the outskirts of the seaside town and emerging on the other side, onto a pier that jutted out into Loch Ryan. They alighted and were directed by barriers through a portacabin. In this building, police were stopping passengers at random to search their luggage. Dillon had prepared him for this and had also given him an address of a fictitious friend in Belfast to cite in the event that he was questioned. In spite of these precautions he was relieved when he was waved through. He decided not to wait for Dillon, but to board the ferry. His companion joined him at the rail that ran around the passenger deck a few minutes afterwards.

Peter, still wishing to conduct their sojourn together on the most pleasant of terms possible, greeted him and then said, ''I was worried about you. I mean, I was wondering whether you still had the gun with you and how you would have got it through.''

Dillon replied simply, ''Coals to Newcastle.'' They arrived in Larne and after clearing the security checks there boarded an N.I.R. train for Belfast. On this occasion the security check was conducted by the Royal Ulster Constabulary. Peter noticed that over their uniforms they were all wearing a thick blue tabard that proffered protection against bullets and shrapnel from explosions. Some of them had black leather straps strung from their shoulders to carry short nosed sub machine guns. Others who required to work with their hands free had pistol holsters attached to their waistbands. Had anyone asked Peter before this trip whether or not, he knew that the R.U.C. was the only police force in Britain whose officers were armed as a matter of routine, he would have told them that of course he did. Witnessing weapons so prominently displayed in a public place for the first time, however, forced him to translate his intellectual appreciation of this fact into a realisation of the dangers of the situation in which he now found himself. It was not a painless metamorphosis.

When they came out of the station Dillon hailed a taxi and directed the driver to "Murphy's Bar", Donegal Quay. Peter had overheard this and thought it a strange destination, but it was explained to him that this would allow them somewhere reasonably comfortable to wait whilst a phone call was made to make further transport arrangements. Dillon was evidently known in the bar for without the need for any words to be passed, a phone was taken from under the bar and placed in front of him as soon as he came in. He pointed to a vacant table and chairs and invited Peter to sit down whilst he made the call. An unsolicited glass of whisky was brought over to the table and he was joined by his travelling companion a minute or so later.

"Drink up if you want it. Our lift will be here very shortly."

Peter took a large gulp and put the glass down. It seemed to be no sooner than he had done so, that a large man in a black donkey jacket came in, touched Dillon on the shoulder and left without uttering a syllable. Dillon's beckoning finger indicated that they should follow. When they got out of the pub Peter was surprised to see an old van parked with both nearside wheels up on the pavement. A driver was nursing the idling engine. The side panel flew open and Dillon roughly pushed Peter inside. Another man was standing there in a crouched position and he pointed to the dirty wooden bench that ran along one side of the van's interior. Peter sat down. Dillon joined him closing the side panel as he entered and the van drove off. The windows at the rear had been covered with black paper which was Sellotaped to the doors. There was no direct access to the front of the van and consequently the only light was that provided by an electric bulb which had been rigged to the roof.

"Call me a snob but I had expected a bit more salubrious transport than this." Peter remarked in a joking tone but also hoping for an explanation for the choice of vehicle.

Dillon gave him this. "I told you the rules are

different over here. I'm going to have to blindfold you in a minute and if any of the security forces looked through the window of a saloon car and saw a blindfolded man being driven through the streets of Belfast, well goodness knows what they might think.''

Then the other passenger passed Dillon a large piece of thick cloth. Dillon put his finger in the air and rotated it, indicating his desire for Peter to stand up and turn around. The blindfold was passed over his eyes and then tied tightly. The unidentified man then said to Peter, ''Hands behind your back.''

Peter followed this instruction more out of a sense of fear than of rational decision making. He felt metal bracelets being clamped to his wrists and struggled. He was no match for the strength of the arms that now pinned his and he heard the click as the handcuffs were locked into place by another pair of hands.

''Hey, is this really necessary, Dillon!.''

The other voice replied, ''Mr Dillon to you.''

''That's O.K Stuart. Mr Sullivan is just a little apprehensive that's all. I'm sure that he doesn't mean to be rude.''

Then Dillon continued to address Peter. ''It's only another of our little precautions. Just in case you suddenly felt the urge to remove the blindfold. It wont be for long.''

Peter was helped to regain his seated position but was still thrown from side to side as he was taken through the streets of the city. Had he been able to observe the route that he followed, he would have noticed that the van went up a long straight hill. Streets of low red brick built houses ran to meet this hill. Towards the top, all of the gable ends were embellished with graffiti of varying levels of artistry. The most elaborate of them was composed of a picture of King William III sitting astride his white charger with his unsheathed sword pointing forward. The words 'Lest we forget' had been painted above this figure and below it was given the information, 'You are now entering Protestant West Belfast'.

Chapter 16

The van stopped and Dillon said, "O.K. Peter just come along where I guide you." Peter was aware of coming out of the vehicle, climbing stairs and going over a doorstep. He seemed to go through two rooms before Dillon helped him down to a chair. It was a hard seat without armrests. He heard the door being shut and became conscious through the sound of low muttering and shuffling feet that a small crowd was now assembled. After the shuffling of feet had finished, he felt the blindfold being untied. He blinked as his eyes became accustomed again to light and could see in front of him a tall grey haired man probably in his early sixties. He wore a conventional pin striped business suit and in appearance could have been mistaken for a bank manager or a solicitor. A wave of relief swept over Peter when he picked up the benign smile. The gesture of warmth and friendship was returned. The captive visitor tried to bring his hands around to his front but learned that they were still secured. He tried again in the hope that somebody would notice his efforts and recognise the discomfort in which he now floundered. This would surely lead to his release before he was compelled to demean himself by asking. The older gentleman appreciated the meaning of this unspoken request at once and demonstrated the spurious nature of his welcome, "I think we'll leave the cuffs on for just now, Mr Sullivan.''

Peter's surprise at hearing this paled in comparison to the jolt he received as he looked around the room. A large Union Jack hung on the wall in front of him. Across its middle ran the slogan 'No Surrender'. He craned his neck and saw on one of the side walls a poster. Two white flags hung from speared poles over a picture of King William. At the top of the poster the words 'Home Rule Is Rome Rule' and, at its bottom, the entreaty 'Orangemen Unite' were read by Peter to himself. He also noticed that beside the man in front of him who had just spoken and Dillon at his side, there were three other men in the room. His mouth opened to start the process of objection and query but no words were uttered. The older gentleman spoke again, ''Welcome to Northern Ireland, Mr Sullivan. I hope that you had a comfortable trip across the water and that our Mr Dillon was looking after you. Have you been to the Emerald Isle before, Mr Sullivan?''

In spite of the deliberate and exaggerated use of his name, Peter did not hear the question. He was still lost within his own confusion. He felt that the shocking paradox would be explained to him in the very near future and all would make sense. The next statements, however threw him deeper into the labyrinth of mental chaos.

''My apologies, Mr Sullivan. I really should have introduced myself first. My name's McLean;

Commander McLean of the Ulster Freedom Fighters. You may have heard of us. We are the only properly constituted force that's not prepared to compromise in any way on maintaining the civil and religious liberties of the Protestant majority of Ulster."

Not only did the content seem incredible, but the method of delivery of the statement, akin to a reading aloud from a political tract, also added to the dreamlike quality of the moment. Confused, he shook his head in the hope that this would awaken him from the nightmare, but found himself still confronted with a horrible reality. Peter shifted in his seat in an effort to acquire some sense of his surroundings. The room appeared dingy and a musty smell that was vaguely redolent of the aroma that is a mixture of stale tobacco smoke and unconsumed alcohol assailed his nostrils. He recognised it easily. It was the same smell that greeted him those mornings that he opened up the pub. Its familiarity almost seemed surprisingly soothing. The walls and ceiling had been covered with a yellowish paint that had taken on a dirty hue from the nicotine stains. The captive's eyes, in as large an arc as his restrictions would permit, followed an elaborate plaster cornice that circumscribed the top of the walls. It had indubitably been once a tribute to the skill of the tradesmen who completed the decoration of this room but was now broken in several places and seemed to be far more compatible with the rest of the decor than its original pretensions.

A grey flex hung from the ceiling and carried the bare electric light bulb that was responsible for most of the illumination in this chamber. Another thin shaft of natural light did shine out in front of him and he guessed that the window would be directly behind him. Putting trust in another sense, he strained his ears for sounds that might give him a clue as to his whereabouts. The silence from the street below and the memory of those twisting turns in rapid succession during the very last part of his journey confirmed a growing fear that he was so deep in the warren of the backstreets of the city that to all intents and purposes he was as alone with these men as he would have been had they been the sole survivors of a shipwreck in the most inhospitable and isolated seas of the world.

He desperately sought the solution to this bizarre puzzle and looked for the questions that would guide him to an answer. Instead the same dumbfounded quizzical look and silence were again the only responses that Peter could muster. McLean took the opportunity to continue in sarcastic, mocking tones, ''You are surprised. You thought that you would be meeting people from the other side of the divide. You expected to arrive at a house somewhere up the Falls Road. Well, Mr Sullivan I wonder what could have happened. Could Mr

Dillon have brought you by mistake to the wrong place? That would have been really unfortunate and remiss of him. Did you make a mistake with your geography, John?"

Dillon smiled, "No Commander. This is definitely the right place."

"Well if this is the right place Mr Sullivan, or can I call you Peter, if this is the right place, then the only explanation for the confusion is that it is us with whom you have been doing business all these years. And very grateful, we are too for all your support."

At last Peter spoke in a plaintive voice, "But Dillon told me that he was in the I.R.A."

McLean waved an admonishing finger at him, "Now I hope that he didn't say that. I agree that he may have led you to believe that he was collecting for the Republican cause."

He turned again to Dillon, "Did you do that wee ditty about Ireland losing its children, in Mr Sullivan's pub?"

Dillon nodded and McLean continued, "Sentimental drivel, but the people love it particularly when they have a drink in them. You've got a great word for that mood over there in Glasgow. You call it 'maudlin'. Have you come across that word Peter?"

Peter nodded, too amazed at the revelation now being unfolded to prevent McLean from continuing.

"We have to make pretensions to the Republican cause because folk are just not prepared to put their hands deep enough into their pockets to support us. But the Taigs, the world over, they get the sympathy vote and they get the money as well. You know what I think Peter? I think its down to sheer complacency." He repeated this idea as though talking to himself 'sheer complacency', and then continued.

"Some of our supporters, particularly outside Ulster think that since we were given a separate state in 1921 to recognise our particular needs we have nothing to worry about. They don't realise just how precarious our freedom really is. You saw what happened with the peace movement, it fizzled out when the I.R.A. realised that it might just be exerting some influence over the Catholic population. The I.R.A. even started a civil war in the South when it realised that some of their countrymen were preparing to let us live in peace. They are an insidious disease. They will continue to wage war until they have us under papist domination. We are besieged as much today as we were at Londonderry's walls or The Boyne. And one day the British Government might just think that enough is enough and sell us down the river. They would forget all the brave Ulstermen who died in wars keeping their island free. For their sake and for the sake of all those who don't want to live under a rule that imposes the edicts of the priest of Rome into the state constitution, we have to be ready to fight."

The effect of this speech on Peter was to allow him to compose his thoughts. As soon as McLean stopped, he asked, "What's all that got to do with me. I'm just a publican from Glasgow, I'm not a threat to you."

"No, Peter you're not a threat to us. You really are a great help. You have provided us with quite tidy sum over the years that will be well used when the final struggle comes. We shall have to fight then for the very ground on which we have lived for generations, for the very beliefs that we have held for centuries."

Peter listened to these fulminations and thought that the Commander must be quite mad. His terror let his tongue slip, "You're off your heads the lot of you. Let me go. I don't want anything to do with this. Take your money and that's us all finished."

He sprang out of the chair and started to turn around to talk to Dillon, but before he completed this action, he felt a heavy blow being delivered to the back of his head. He would have sunk to the floor had he not been supported by a net of arms and placed again on his seat. The Commander lifted his chin and spoke gently to him. "It has got to do with everyone, Peter. No-one who has any connection with this Province in any way, shape or form is innocent. You would willingly have let that money be passed into the hands of common murderers and terrorists. There would have been deaths on your conscience had Mr Dillon not intervened. You should perhaps be grateful to him.''

''But if you're not the I.R.A. why did Dillon pull a gun on those Rangers supporters that day, and what about the one you beat up?''

The Commander looked at Dillon, ''Perhaps you would explain it to our friend here.''

Dillon walked around to face Peter. ''It was all an illusion just like the letter and the telephone number. It's just a terrible pity that you had to insist on playing the big man and demanding that you come across to see for yourself. Well now my friend you have seen. You know everything there is to know and that's not good news for you.''

''But I even checked the story about the guy in Larkhall in my copy of the newspaper'', snapped Peter.

''Yes I know you did. I was impressed at that. But the man that we kneecapped that day was nowhere near the ''Derry Bar''. The boys that came in then all worked for us. It was a set up. It was even a dummy gun. You can't carry a real pistol about you know, that only happens in gangster films. They had all been primed to beat it when I made my move. And the guy who got kneecapped, well he was one of us but then he deserted. He had been given a job to do and then changed his mind about helping us. He was always going to be punished. We just waited for a time that would suit other purposes as well."

Peter was amazed. He said, "But he was called Ronnie, the same name as the guy in the pub who head butted me and you got his address through the registration number."

McLean interrupted, "Come now Mr Sullivan, think about it. I doubt very much whether your assailant was really called 'Ronnie'. That was the name of the man that Mr Dillon would be chastising and I imagine that he asked one of his associates to assume it so that it would tie up with the newspaper reports. Correct Mr Dillon?"

"Absolutely, Commander."

He returned to addressing Peter, "And the registration number got thrown in the bucket because I already had Ronnie's address, but it was a nice little touch letting you think we were in cahoots with the peelers".

Peter looked angry. The realisation of just how much he had been tricked was dawning on him. All of these years Dillon had duped him, fooled him, lied to him and stole from him. In one swift stroke the image that he held tightly of himself had not just been knocked from its pedestal but had been shattered into so many fragments that he doubted whether they could ever be fixed together again into a form that would be recognised as worthy of possession. As he realised how foolish this pretence would make him seem in the eyes of others he shook his head. His anger spilled over into his question to McLean.

"Are you telling me that you are not murderers and terrorists?"

"I wouldn't be so self righteous as to tell you that, Peter. But we only exist as a counter balance to other forces. Were it to be made quite clear that that superstitious ridden Republic had no claims on us and if the Catholics up here either accepted it or went South, then we would cease to be. We fight fire with fire but I don't see these brave men as terrorists. We are more of a counter terrorist organisation. Heroes for the Unionist cause."

Peter was not prepared to argue the fine semantics of this point. He was concerned with his own position, "So what are you going to do to me? I'm not one of your enemies."

"I'm afraid that you are, Peter. You are not with us, at least not that you knew, so you must be against us. Mr Dillon did warn you how dangerous this trip would be so you have arrived at this point through your own free will, or is it Calvin's argument about predestination?"

The Commander laughed at his own little digression. He went into a drawer of the desk behind him and took out a pistol. As soon as Peter saw this he let loose a scream of terror and again jumped out of the seat. This time he recognised Dillon's face behind the punch that knocked him to the floor. Two other men then helped him to a kneeling position with his chin tightly held against the edge of the desk. Whilst this was happening the Commander walked to the window, looked out and slowly came back. He was oblivious to the violence in front of him. After a few minutes he spoke again in the same deliberate tones.

"Mr Sullivan, it matters not a jot to this organisation how much you scream. The neighbours have a very selective deafness to the sounds that come from this house. I have to say though that I personally find the howling of a grown man most disconcerting. If you shout out like that again before we are finished this most interesting discussion, then my colleague over there has an electric cow prod and I shall ask him to remove your trousers and insert it up your arse. You will then have every reason in the world to scream."

" What are you going to do to me? Please let me go."

"No. I'm afraid that letting you go just yet is not an option. These other gentlemen here all think that they know now what I'm going to do. They think that I'm going to kill you. And its very important Peter that you are in no doubt that killing you is an easy way of concluding this rather strange business. I could shoot you. I could have you taken through to the bath tub next door and have you drowned. I've killed other men who mean a lot more to me than you. An awful lot more, I can assure you.''

Peter felt his face being thrust deeper into the wood of the desk. His arms were now held so tightly that they burned. Someone roughly grabbed a handful of his hair and twisted his head around so that he could not prevent himself from looking at the Commander. He saw the pistol being placed at the back of his neck.

He shouted out ''Please God, no!'' and heard a click as the hammer sprung back. All of a sudden he felt himself being released from the pressures that had restrained him. His body slunk slowly to the floor and he thought he could feel warm urine trickling down his leg. The warmth was strangely pleasant and comforting. He became aware that he was crying and could not open his eyes because of the sting of the tears. Then his father was helping him to his feet. James Sullivan was with him in that room more real than any of the others. Peter not only saw his father but could feel his presence as well. The genuinenesss of the presence was totally convincing.

''Come on son. Wipe your eyes. You're a good boy.''

''Oh, Dad. What will I do? They've really screwed me. What am I going to do? Help me Dad. Help me, please.''

''You will be alright. I'm here now. Just remember what I've told you. Surviving's the most important thing. What we did to survive in business is what brought you here. Now you've got to survive this."

Peter then felt a sharp kick on the ribs that reminded him in a very certain way that he was still lying on the floor.

"C'mon up, up to the seat, you bastard", he heard one of the strange voices say. He was helped and after a moment felt that the tears had subsided sufficiently to allow him to open his eyes. The faces were all laughing at him. He thought very briefly that it might have been better had he been killed. He thought of blackness and then appreciated the preciousness of life. The Commander continued his conversation as though there had been no interruption.

"But they were of no use to me, these other men. You are different, Peter. You could continue to be of service to us. We would like our little financial arrangement to continue and that of course would require you to be there. So killing you would be a bit like cutting off our nose to spite our face. But I have to tell you that should you breathe a word of this to a living soul, then I would kill you without blinking an eyelid. Mr Dillon will accompany you back to Glasgow and introduce you to another of our agents, a Mr Timms, who will take over the collections. Mr Dillon is to get another posting in recognition of all his good work over there."

Had Peter the inclination to look at Dillon he would have seen surprise register on his face at this news.

"Now listen carefully, this will serve as a warning. But should you renege from our arrangement or not follow Mr Timm's instructions to the letter, then I'll have you killed as well. Straight away, no messing about this time, no meeting to discuss it or iron out any misunderstandings. It's the bullet straight away. Do you understand that?"

Peter nodded before the Commander went back to his admonitions.

"If you try to get the drop on us by having Mr Timms harmed in any way, then my vengeance will be wreaked not only on you but on all of your family. I'm not just talking about Mrs Sullivan, here, but your brothers and sisters will also get a bullet. I'll ensure, though, that you suffer a particularly gruesome death. Maybe we'll drop you from the top of a multi-storey. You do believe me, don't you Mr Sullivan?"

His heart was pounding violently but his over riding feeling was one of relief now that he knew there was a probable alternative outcome to being murdered in a dingy flat somewhere in the back streets of Belfast. He had no doubts though about both the Commander's sincerity and capability of carrying out this threat. The image of his father again briefly entered his head. He recalled that time in the pub where he had been urged to make all of his business decisions in the light of how much they would contribute to his livelihood. It all seemed so incredibly clear to him now. He looked up at the Commander and spoke in a voice, the calmness of which surprised himself.

"Yes I believe you. And I'm not going to put my life at risk again. The collections will continue in the "Derry Bar". I'll do what you want and Mr Timms has nothing to fear from me."

"Good", exclaimed the Commander obviously pleased with this response. "But don't be too hard on yourself. We have this scam running in Liverpool, London and lots of places in the States and Canada. In fact the only place we can't run it is Ireland because it would be too easy to check out the agents. Isn't that rather ironical? You're certainly not the only one to be taken in you know. So don't feel too bad about yourself, Peter."

Now that fear had dissipated, curiosity raised its head.

"But what if the genuine I.R.A. boys are actually there already or turn up later on?"

"Now, we've had that little upset over in Boston fairly recently. By all accounts there was a terrible confusion that night. 'Would the real I.R.A. man, please stand up?' It must have been a little like one of these television panel games. But of course he didn't have any more credentials than our man.

So there was a stand off that night. It just meant we had to temporarily close down our operation there and remove our agent in case the reprisals got out of hand.''

Peter was now completely composed. He even managed a smile as he said, ''I have to hand it to you, it's a pretty clever trick''.

The Commander nodded his appreciation of the compliment.

''We think so too. It's like having our offspring fed in someone else's nest. We are very fond of ornithological allusions here. We think of you as the goose that lays the golden eggs, and this little ruse we call, the 'Cuckoo Plot'.''

Chapter 17

The prisoner and an entourage of guards left the room to make their way on the journey that would allow Peter to escape the madness that tormented his mind. The scar of the afternoon's events would be with him forever but that he had the ability to recall them was a blessing to him. He had once heard the phrase 'Hanging concentrates the mind wonderfully' and had thought it to be one of the most nonsensical things ever said to him. As he came out of the doorway and felt himself being assisted into the van, he ascribed the words an almost mystical, esoteric significance.

The Commander was now with only Dillon and Norris. He looked at his lieutenant.

"You had better check that these wee urchins haven't taken the fucking wheels off the car. Bring it round to the front. We'll be going as soon as I have a word with your man, here."

As Norris departed McLean explained to Dillon that he had given some money to a few children of the street to watch his car.

"Can't get too much security in our game, John."

"I think that's another example of you going soft, Commander. You know that no one around here would dare even look at your motor, never mind steal it."

"Perhaps you're right. What's the first example of me going soft? Letting Sullivan go? Is that what's hurting you, John? Has your pride been dented somehow, eh? Do you think I'm forcing you to cow tow to your man there?"

The Commander had straightened himself and was a good half a head taller than Dillon. The truculence in his voice was unmistakeable. He would try to intimidate by virtue of the difference of the physical size of the two men, but Dillon held his stare. He realised that the Commander had given him leave to speak his mind by arranging that only the two of them should occupy the room at this time and would not let slip the opportunity. He could not, however, summon up the words that would allow him to fire an opening salvo in this battle of wills. The commander won the war of attrition. Dillon blinked and dropped the guard of the stare. Then he could only see the symbols of authority that had directed all of his adult life.

"I was surprised enough to learn about the transfer that you had lined up for me, but when I heard you tell that bastard that he could walk out of here....." He hesitated, that expression of consternation came again to his face. He had run out of words, his only option was to retrace his steps from this verbal dead-end and find another way of articulating his concerns.

"Surely we can't allow him to go home. He

183

knows about us, he knows about me." The voice tapered off and any barb that had been attached to the tone when Dillon first challenged the Commander disappeared into the ether.

The contest that McLean had expected had now completly evaporated. His potential adversary contended his position in an apologetic fashion. He was seeking an explanation not a reversal of the decision.

"Don't worry, John. Nothing will happen to you. You are one of our best men. If I thought for one second that you would be in danger, I would have shot Sullivan myself. He's like a rabbit though, caught in the headlights of a car. He's paralysed by fright. There's absolutely no way he will do anything but continue to give us the money that we need. I give you my word on that. Anyway you are going to have a wee break with your dad and then its off to Boston. You fly from Gatwick in a fortnight's time."

The last time that Dillon had lain in bed with Isabel, flitted through his mind. Their relationship had lasted for over three years which was longer than his ill-fated marriage. Only now, in this moment in which his world received unchallengeable directions to change course, did the full force of the futility of the relationship strike him, a futility that in reality had existed for as long as their relationship.

"I have to go back to Glasgow just for a short time. I need to say 'cheerio' to Gerry. He's been a good friend to me, particularly when Jim died. I've also got to pick up a few personal things. That wont be a problem will it?''

''Not at all. I want you to introduce Sullivan to Gerry, remember. Your Dad's expecting you tonight though. That's why we have stuck the bold boy up in the ''Dunaddry''. It'll be handy for Antrim, we thought. One of the lads will run you up tonight and collect you in the morning to take you and Sullivan to the boat.''

The Commander opened the door and continued, ''Your car should be waiting downstairs. Give my best regards to your Dad''.

The conversation had been brought to an end. A sweep of the Commander's hand indicated that Dillon should leave first.

As he passed he said, ''Christ it's not going to be a Sunday school picnic taking Sullivan back to Scotland.''

''I'm sure it'll be no harder than when you thought you were bringing him over to be executed.''

At the street, Dillon was met by Norris who fell in step with him as he walked to the other side of the road and a waiting car. A thick brown paper bag the sort used by licensed grocers to wrap up cans of beer was thrust into Dillon's stomach.

''This will not be as hard to swallow as the Commander's decision to let him go.''

The beneficiary laughed but as his hands ran

over the outside of the bag, he did not feel the cylindrical shapes he associated with this type of container and the smile turned to a tight grimace. The curves were unmistakable. He felt first the barrel, then the handle and by folding the excess paper up he could locate the trigger with his finger. The explanation was delivered surreptitiously out of the side of Norris's mouth and in whispered tones.

"It's long enough and quiet enough on the roads that Jimmy will take between the "Dunaddry" and the boat for you to do the business."

The Commander appeared and watched as Dillon and Norris shook hands. He started to drum his fingers impatiently on top of the car that was now parked directly outside the entrance to the common stair from which he had emerged. When this was deliberately ignored he shouted on his lieutenant and then with a pointed finger directed Dillon to the car in front. The Commander and Norris sat in silence together in the back seat as their car followed Dillon's out of the side streets, onto the main road and downhill, with Belfast Lough always in sight. At the bottom of St. Peter's Street the convoy split.

Mclean had waited for this moment to speak, almost as though he feared that he would be overheard for as long as the two cars remained in sight of one another. Now he could triumphantly reveal to his captive audience the last part of his secret. He shifted around and beckoned Norris to move closer before he said in a whispered voice.

"Are you wondering why I'm so confident about letting Sullivan go."

"I presume it's because that if we did him in that would be the end of the 'Cuckoo Plot' in the "Derry Bar", and I know the idea is your baby."

"Aye, it probably would be the end. Maybe not just in the "Derry Bar" either, but there's another more important reason."

Both speaker and driver desperately wanted to break the silence that ensued, but both were determined that it should be the other one that would do so. At last the silent tension forced Norris to capitulate. He said in tones that he hoped would give no indication that he realised that he had just lost another contest.

"And what would that other reason be, Commander?"

"I knew the boy's father. I knew old man Sullivan. Away back in 1946 I had just completed my first year at Queen's when I got a summer job labouring in a building site over in Scotland. There was another Irishman working there, James Sullivan. It didn't matter a hoot to the rest of the squad that he was a Tim and I was a Proddy, we were both thick Paddies. But do you know it didn't matter to Sullivan either. He sort of took me under his wing. He said he had never known a Proddy cooley before. We used to have our cup of tea together and the odd pint. I spent two months with that man hauling hods of bricks up and down ladders and shovelling shit all over the place. I was determined to let him see that the Protestants of Ireland were as proud of being Irish as he was. He just laughed when I said that and told me that it was his intention to take money from everyone. Then he told me about this idea he had about running an Irish bar in Glasgow. He even said that as long as I kept my trap shut about religion and an Irish accent in my head I could come and work for him. But I tell you that the idea had nothing to do with being proud of being Irish, it was the man's way of getting out of the building site. He said time and time again that this idea would do for him and his family what university would do for me. So when I heard that we were working over the ''Derry Bar'' and that it belonged to Sullivan's son, I reckoned that the boy would be imbued with the same sense of values and priorities as his old man. As long as we don't completely ruin him, he'll be happy enough to let us continue gathering in the money.''

Chapter 18

Just as he was leaving that flat in Belfast, the Commander had explained to Peter that he would be driven to the ''Dunaddry'' Hotel, Templepartick, where a reservation had been made in his name.

''I thought that you would prefer to leave Belfast straight away after our little chat and the ''Dunaddry'' is a nice place to spend the night. Far enough away to help you forget your little fright but close enough to us, to remember my message.''

Peter had nodded his appreciation of the Commander's forethought and sensitivity to his wishes. He thought that these qualities were strangely compatible with his insanity, but insane he most certainly was. The Commander had continued to tell him that Dillon would pick him up mid morning and they would be in Larne in time for the midday sailing.

''But just before you leave us, I believe you have a little message for me.''

Peter pulled out of his inside jacket pocket an envelope that contained the money he had been told he owed them. The Commander thanked him so profusely that the words and gestures seemed almost grotesquely sycophantic. Then with a complete and sudden contrast of moods he gestured to one of his aides to replace the blindfold. Peter felt himself being led back to the van. When he was transferred to a saloon car, the blindfold was removed and he could see seagulls flying overhead. He could also smell the distinct scent of salt water and calculated that he had again been brought to the docks area.

He found himself alone with the driver but neither man had any inclination to engage the other in discussion. As a consequence the half-hour journey was undertaken in complete silence.

The "Dunaddry" comprised of one long white single storey building, sitting in its own grounds. Peter noted that before they could enter, the car was subjected to a security search, but felt that this was conducted in a rather perfunctory manner and that should anyone really have wanted to smuggle in guns or a bomb, it would not present them with too great a challenge. The car proceeded and then stopped outside the front door and the driver, still without speaking, jerked his thumb at the back seat. Peter saw his overnight case there and reached to get it. He found it awkward to shut the door of the car without saying 'cheerio' or 'thank you'. But he succeeded. The driver in turn stared motionlessly at the white building in front of him. As soon as the door was slammed shut, the car sped off. Peter chose not to watch its departure but instead strode purposefully inside.

He signed the register and was directed to his room. To reach the bedroom, Peter had to pass through the bar area. As he was negotiating his way around the tables, he decide that he would benefit from a stiff drink. He approached the young barman with the sickly smiling face, and ordered a whisky.

"Scotch or Irish, sir?"

Peter felt that he would like to have punched him straight in the face but simply glowered before replying, "Scotch. A large one."

He drank it quickly, went to his room and lay down on the bed. He had to rise two minutes later and just reached the toilet pan as he started to vomit. The sweat was still pouring out of his forehead, when he picked up the phone and asked the receptionist how far he was from Larne.

"Oh, about half an hour by car." came the startled response.

"Good, will you get me the Ferry company please."

"Sealink or P. and O, sir?"

"Just get me the one that will get me to Stranraer, will you?" barked Peter. As soon as he had replaced the receiver, he regretted his outburst of bad temper at this innocent bystander to his sorry experience. Then he remembered the Commander's contention that there were no innocents. He had no time to ponder this point before the telephone rang and a voice informed him, "Sealink Larne. Booking and reservations here".

He discovered that there was a ferry sailing at 9 pm in three hours time. Although he knew a booking had been made in his name for the following day, Dillon had the ticket. He decided not to waste time trying to arrange a transfer and requested a reservation for the late evening crossing. He then asked reception to make up his bill and get him a taxi.

"Something unexpected, sir?" said the young girl at the front desk with the smart skirt, the white blouse and fixed smile, when he came back down with his case. He wondered why the staff in this hotel had to look so bloody pleased with themselves.

"Yes, very unexpected, indeed."

Peter tried to eat a meal on board the ferry but found that he had no stomach for food. The boat docked at Stranraer just shortly after midnight. He asked one of the uniformed policemen on security duty to recommend a good hotel and was directed to the North-West Castle.

"Just across the road and next to the police station. He found that strangely reassuring or he wondered was it simply because he was back in Scotland that the sense of panic was decreasing. The large oak revolving doors had been locked, but a bell at the side provided a means of summoning attention. He explained his late arrival and lack of a booking to the night porter by telling him that he had to come back from a business trip in a bit of a hurry.

It had been a long exhausting day but he did not sleep. He lay restlessly fully dressed on top of the bed. The ordeal of the previous day was replayed over and over in the cinema of his mind. At the end of each of these performances he asked himself how he could have been so stupid as to be taken in by Dillon. He decided that he would never tell anyone what he had learned. It seemed that the only greater humiliation he could suffer was for the world to know that he was a fool. He specifically included for different reasons, Ann and Isabel in these thoughts.

As soon as the morning light penetrated his room, he showered and went downstairs. He decided to skip breakfast and make immediate plans for his return to Glasgow. He learned that the first train was not till much later that morning and decided to make the ninety mile trip home by taxi. Peter told the driver that he would have to get the cash for the fare from inside his house when they arrived. This did not seem to be a problem and the driver tried hard to pass the journey by instigating conversation. His passenger was more reticent, however, and replied only as far as basic courtesy demanded.

As they drove through familiar streets towards the end of their journey, Peter's feeling of unease and discomfort started to return. Just before they were about to turn up the drive of his house, he asked the driver to pull over. He enquired whether he would be prepared to accept a cheque instead of cash for the fare. When he replied that he would, Peter gave him Ann's address. The door of the tenement flat was knocked tentatively.

It was only half past nine in the morning and he

was unsure not just if he would be welcome but whether Ann would be out of bed. Ann answered the door and looked at him for a moment. She was dressed in an old house coat that had stains arranged in patterns down its front. She looked as though she had been awake all night; there were black circles around her eyes and her skin seemed puffed up. Peter winced when he looked at her. The prospect of spending time with her did not seem so exciting as it had done only a few minutes, previously. Suddenly she shouted, "You're alright, that's great. Come in."

Her arms simultaneously locked around his neck. The surprise of this statement precipitated a surge of adrenaline that allowed him to break her grip of affection with ease and push her back into the flat. He followed and shut the door behind him.

"Why shouldn't I be alright? Why did you ask me that?"

He couldn't separate his feelings of confusion from an anger over the notion that she could possibly be aware of his recent experience. She detected the notes of pain in his voice and led him through to the kitchen. She started to ask whether he wished a cup of tea or coffee, but he interrupted.

"For fuck's sake never mind that the now. Tell me why you asked me if I was alright."

She rushed into the explanation as though it was a task that had to be completed before more enjoyable activities could be undertaken.

"I didn't believe you last week when you said you were going over to Belfast. I just had a feeling that you were kidding me the night you told me that you worked for the I.R.A. So I thought that I would phone up your house. I expected you to answer it. But a woman picked up the phone and asked who I was. Was that your wife?"

The question held a particular irrelevance for Peter, but he managed to contain his irritation long enough to confirm her guess.

"I expect it was. What did you say?"

"Nothing, believe me. I didn't tell her anything about us. I knew you were married that first night we came back here so I'm not complaining."

"Ann, tell me why you thought I had been harmed." Peter's frustration was growing.

"Well, I told her that I was just a friend and she said that if I was one of your cheap tarts I should know that you weren't coming back. I asked her what she meant and she said something about the cheating bastard had been taken care of. Oh! Peter, I didn't know what to think. I was really worried. Honestly I was."

Ann had managed to get her arms around his neck again and Peter was finding this uncomfortable. She had started to sob, a low rhythmic sob, that increased Peter's regret that he had chosen to come to see her.

"I have to go."

"You'll come back though, wont you? You can stay here if you like. Did your wife try to kill you?"

He stopped in his tracks and turned this last question over in his mind. He had been wrestling in his mind to solve the puzzle of how Isabel could have known about the danger that he had faced and the prospect of him not returning. The solution had been so obvious but he had refused to recognise it until Ann had thrown it into his face. He walked out without answering either of her questions.

It had started to drizzle and now that Autumn was turning, Peter felt a distinct chill in the air. He had no coat and was still carrying his small case. In spite of this he decided to walk. Images of days like these when he had come back from school and dried off in front of the large open fire in the tenement flat, flooded his mind. He could remember the feelings of anticipation awaiting his father's return from work, particularly on a Friday when he would usually bring home a couple of bars of Fry's Five Boys to share out. The descriptions of the faces on the wrapper would then be attributed to his father's perception of the moods of his children. More often than not Peter's would be 'anticipation'.

The wet and the cold were uncomfortable on his bare head. His jacket soon became heavy with moisture. This all felt good to him. It reminded him he was alive. He walked the three or so miles from Bridgeton to Burnside. When he turned into his drive the first sight that caught his eye was Isabel loading a suitcase into the boot. She was aware that the Andersons were watching her but she failed to turn around to see Peter. She was also too preoccupied with her own thoughts to hear his footsteps on the gravel until he was close enough to say, "Hello Isabel.......Are you leaving me now?"

"Oh Holy Jesus! What are you doing here? I mean you startled me. I didn't expect you."

"No Isabel. I hear that you didn't expect me at all. This must be a pleasant surprise for you."

"So you've already spoken to your little whore, have you? You fucking worm."

"Don't bother changing the subject just now. Tell me why you told her that I wouldn't be coming back. Tell me, Isabel"

As he had spoken he had grabbed her wrist and was holding it tightly. She struggled and the Andersons lifted the window so that they could hear the exchanges.

"Let me go you bastard. Why did they muck it up? They will kill you the next time."

"So you knew what was going to happen, you fucking bitch. You tried to have me killed did you? Why? why? why?"

"Because I love Dillon. I'll still have you killed."

It felt as though a bucket of ice cold water had been thrown into Peter's face. The shock was such that he had to gasp for breath. He instinctively released Isabel's wrist and she ran into the house. He chased her, caught up with her in the hall and slapped her face. She put her hand up to cover her pain and then returned his slap with greater force. Peter screamed at her, closed his fist and punched her on the side of her head with sufficient strength to knock her to the floor. He continued to hurl abuse at her but when he had exhausted his immediate supply of suitable descriptions of derision, he asked her.

"What could Dillon give you that I haven't? Look at the house, at your clothes. You don't want for anything. What could he give you?"

She looked up at him but still cowering and said, "A baby. I'm pregnant and it's his."

Peter froze. For a few seconds nothing in the world moved as this news percolated into his consciousness. He then went meekly into the lounge and sat down. As soon as he had stopped standing over her, Isabel quickly climbed to her feet and ran to the kitchen. She stood with her back barring the door lest he decided to chase her and hit her again. In one of the drawers she searched for and found the large bread knife. Its black wooden handle was gripped tightly and she embraced this instrument that would serve as the leverage to achieve her freedom should her husband again interfere with her escape.

She found him still sitting in his favourite armchair. Beads of moisture covered his face. In the light of the room she was unsure whether they were sweat or rain but his countenance appeared to have found a strange sense of serenity. He turned round to face her and saw the knife.

"You don't need that. I'm not going to stop you, Isabel. We're finished now, everything is well and truly over. As far as I'm concerned you and that Protestant bastard can rot in hell together, if he'll have you."

The arm holding the knife fell to her side. The calmness of his voice seemed to accentuate the clarity of the words.

She said, "What do you mean, Protestant bastard? How can he be a Protestant and work for the I.R.A."

The realisation that Isabel was not aware of Dillon's true allegiances confirmed his belief that she too had been unaware of the trick that had been played on them. He laughed and then he started pointedly to laugh at her.

"Didn't he tell you who he worked for? Didn't he tell you that he has been conning us for all these years. He's a die hard Hun, a Billy. An orange bastard. He's in the fucking U.F.F. not the I.R.A. for God's sake. Did your lover not tell you that or were you too busy being screwed to hear it ? He fucking screwed both of us well and truly. He fucking told me, and while he told me his pals were busy scaring the shit out of me, pretending that they were going to kill me."

Isabel was rocked. From all she knew about Peter this was not the sort of ploy he would use against her for the mere sake of hurting her. And yet it could make no other sense when placed against the backcloth of her love for the father of the unborn child she carried. Her husband's tranquillity, however, kept rising to the surface of the dark water that was her confusion. She tried hard not to hear his words being repeated in her mind but Dillon's statement about not being able to love anyone who did not share the same religion as himself kept ringing in her ears and forced her to listen.

"You're lying", she said defiantly to Peter.

"No I'm not. Why would I lie about that? What would I have to gain now? You could ask him yourself, only he's being transferred out of Glasgow. That leaves you really stuck up the creek doesn't it?"

She looked at his face and knew instinctively that he had spoken the truth. She turned and ran out the door. The keys of the car were still in the lock of the boot. She removed them and drove out onto the street. The Andersons watched her departure. They could not have noticed, however, that Isabel was constantly being distracted by furtive glances towards the passenger seat. On its upholstery lay the bread knife.

Chapter 19

The rain continued for the rest of that day. Isabel drove around the town until she found herself in the vicinity of Dillon's flat. She realised that her unconscious mind had been her guide but did not know why it had brought her here. She turned and drove away, following capricious decisions to take this turn and then that. Again though she recognised streets that were familiar from her visits to her lover's flat. She decided to concede to that instinct within that was leading her.

She parked her car on the other side of the street from the close whose entrance she knew so well. When the engine was turned off and the wipers ceased to operate, the streams of rain that ran down the windscreen blurred her vision. The front windows of the flat remained just visible. The bay window on the left belonged to the shared sitting room and the one on the right with the thin patterned curtains was of Dillon's bedroom. Isabel had often drawn and opened these curtains. She pictured the rather sparsely furnished room inside and wondered whether Dillon was there just now. After a short while she noticed a figure moving around in the front of the sitting room. She was not able to identify the indistinct form.

She decided that just to sit in the car and to hope for some revelation was a futile strategy. She had seen a telephone box on the other side of the block and walked quickly to it but still the wetness penetrated her clothes. Before her new found determination evaporated she dialled the number of the flat and awaited a response. It was Timms voice she heard and she contemplated merely returning the phone to its cradle. But the voice was now repeating its question as to whether anyone was there. She heard herself in the echo of the booth telling him that it was Isabel and enquiring whether John was at home.

"No, I'm sorry Isabel. He's not here just now. I'll take a message for the man if you like."

"No, that's alright, Gerry. It's not important. When do you think he will be back?"

"Probably later on today. He's been in Belfast on business, but he should be back before teatime. Will I get him to phone you tonight?"

Thoughts raced through Isabel's mind. She knew that she had to confront Dillon with her husband's accusation. Some instinct raged up to shout to her that giving him notice of her intent would not be the most astute strategy.

"No, no. Don't bother if he's just back. It's really not that important. I can contact him tomorrow or the next day."

She ran back to the car, sat and waited. Her sense of the rhythm of the passing hours was lost. She was unclear what time it was when the taxi stopped on the other side of the street. Dillon got out and settled the fare through the window. Isabel had once been told that it was only in Glasgow that passengers would pay the taxi driver before alighting. The rest of the world used the routine that her lover was now following. This observation on cultural differences would be the type of trivia that would be passed around the "Derry Bar" and then become a topic worthy of a good hour's conversation. It might then have been relayed to her by her husband on his return home in the delusion that she would share the fascination with such factual clutter. Isabel thought that it was probably apocryphal anyway and tried to dismiss from her mind any significance that she may impart to this recollection. When she had to struggle to do so it occurred to her that she was emphasising to herself that he came from a different place and had a heritage in which she did not share.

Passers-by looked through the windscreen and saw the woman crumpled over the steering wheel. No-one stopped to enquire whether she had suffered from an unexpected illness. Had they done so they would have heard a gentle sobbing. They would not have known, though, that the tears were the result not of what she had recently learned but from a frustration borne from her ignorance of how she should proceed. Her mascara ran down her face and she was aware of what a pitiful sight she must have provided. She looked up feeling at once relieved that she had been the subject of only curiosity rather than Samaritan attentions and yet so alone. Then she saw Timms come out of the close and walk quickly down the street. Later on she would reflect on this moment and wonder why she had taken the knife that still lay on the seat beside her and concealed it in the large inside pocket of her coat. She would not reach an answer with which she could satisfy her desire for comprehension.

As she climbed the stairs and knocked on the door of the flat, she was not aware that she was about to switch on a current that would flow through the chain of events to follow, imparting a charge into each link. These would impact on the whole sequence until the foundations of not only her own world but also those of her husband and lover had been tested and shocked in their own distinct way.

"Isabel, What are you doing here? It's not Friday."

"Can I come in John? I need to talk to you without you making jokes about it not being the right day to see you. I'm fed up of only being able to see you on Fridays."

Dillon held the door tightly, barring her entry.

"It's not really suitable just now. I'm just back and Gerry has gone down to the shops to get something for tea. He'll be back in five minutes or so. Let's meet tomorrow and we can talk then."

Her face was already pale but more blood drained away. This rejection provided irrefutable confirmation of her husband's recent assertions.

"I don't think you will be here tomorrow. Peter told me what happened and who you really are."

It seemed as though Dillon had slipped on a mask when Isabel's gaze had been momentarily diverted. His facial expressions changed dramatically and completely. She had not seen before such looks of anger and astonishment. His stutter had not returned since those early meetings when she had mercilessly teased him. Now it seemed to seek vengeance at its imposed exile.

"What, P ... P .... Peter told you what ha... ha... happened to h.... him?"

"You seem surprised that I know now that you're working for the U.F.F. or whatever you call yourself and that this Catholic pretence was all an act to con money out of Peter. It must have seemed a touch ironical when you got me as well. Had a good laugh at that, have you?"

He realised that she had repeated the detail of her new found information as proof of her possession of it. The door was opened just wide enough to permit access and Isabel did not dance attendance for any more formal invitation. She stood in the hall and awaited his response.

"The reason I'm surprised is that I thought

Peter would want to keep quiet about it. Something about not wanting the world to know about how he was tricked by a gang of thick Paddies. But I should have guessed. It was the same about the gun and the trip over the water. He just can't not tell you. Maybe there's something in your relationship that neither of you really recognise.''

''No, you were right first time. Peter wouldn't have told me. He could have coped eventually with whatever you did to him in Belfast. But the humiliation he would feel from passing you money for the last three years and the idea of people knowing about it, that would be too much. It would be like his father's worries about him coming true.''

''So how do you know about me, then?''

''Because Peter thought it was a way of hurting me when I told him that that humiliation was small beer compared to what you have done to me. ''

''What?''

''You can't guess can you? I'm pregnant. I'm going to have your child.''

Dillon covered his face with both of his hands and screamed at Isabel.

''You fucking stupid bitch. What did you go and do that for? There's no future for the little bastard. You'll have to get rid of it. Do you understand?''

''John, you know that I can't get rid of it. That's like murder. We can go away together, though, and start afresh. The three of us. Somewhere where nobody will know about us. The house and the pub, they don't matter. Peter can rot in hell in them."

"I told you before Isabel, you just don't understand what I'm up against. All my life I've been besieged by the doctrines of the Catholic church. If the U.F.F. wasn't there you Fenians would take over my country. Priests kicked me about when I was a kid at my grandfather's, they're not going to do it again."

Isabel had grabbed him and started to try to shake him. "Don't be a fucking stupid bigot. This has nothing to do with me. Its got nothing to do with the kid I'm carrying. I don't give a damn what happens over there. If that's all that prevents us from being together, I'll stop going to Mass tomorrow. You are more important."

He squeezed her wrists and thrust them downwards breaking her grip on him, before he turned to walk away. As he moved out of the hall he said, "That's what my mother said almost to the word. It didn't work for her and it won't work for you, Isabel. You just proved that with your ideas on abortion. Ask your nuns at Notre Dame where they came from."

"You bastard. You were going to leave anyway. Peter told me you would be leaving Glasgow. When you told me that day you could never love someone who wasn't the same religion as you, you were thinking about me all along. Weren't you?''

Dillon ignored her. He went to his bedroom and took a suitcase down from the top of the wardrobe and started to fill it with clothes from a drawer. He had been followed by Isabel continuing to ask for an answer to her last question. Her persistence was matched by Dillon's resolve not to respond and together these two forces created a spiral of her voice growing louder and louder. When it reached its crescendo, the impasse was broken and she resorted to throwing herself on him in an effort to prevent him packing. He easily fended this off by pushing her away with a thrust that signalled its strength by the loudness of the bang as her head collided with the door frame.

Then Dillon was lying on the floor. He would roll over first this way and then back. The loud yelling had ceased and was replaced by a low almost musical moaning. She was appalled at how much blood had been spilled on the carpet and on the clothes in the suitcase. His hands were bright from his attempts to staunch the wounds himself and the same rich red fluid trickled out of his mouth. Her coat had been splattered and the knife was dripping right up to the hilt. As she became aware of this scene, the knife grew hotter in her hands until it burned her flesh. She dropped it onto the bed and fled.

Chapter 20

Had Isabel's flight been delayed for a mere minute longer, then her departure from the common close would have coincided with Timms' return from the corner grocery shop. As it transpired, however, his anxieties were not raised until he noticed the door to the flat wide open. He shouted to his flat mate and was directed by the sounds of moaning to the bedroom. He had sufficient presence of mind not to ask the questions that were firing themselves into his mouth until he had he raced to the bathroom and returned with towels which he pressed against the leaking wounds.

"What happened? Who did this, John? Can you hear me John? Who did it?"

Dillon's eyes were glassy when they opened and he looked up. Before the cumulative effect of shock and pain and the loss of blood made Dillon lapse into the relief of unconsciousness, he uttered one name to Timms. The effort required to precede it with a Christian name or a title was too great ...... "Sullivan."

Timms swore under his breath and then dialled 999. He explained to the operator that there had been a terrible accident and asked for an ambulance as a matter of urgency. He made sure that she had the correct address and then replaced the receiver. It took only a minute for him to collect the envelope at the bottom of the freezer that contained the four sets of passports and driving licences in the names of Timms, Dillon, Stewart and Marshall. The pistol was hidden under one of the floor boards and this was put in the pocket of his suede leather jacket. He saw the blood still oozing out of his friend's wounds and staining the towels, but knew that he could not stay in the flat any longer. As he made his way to the main road he heard the alarm of the ambulance as it rushed on its mission. Dillon would be in the Western Infirmary in matter of minutes. He also was aware that the Police would be round at the flat as soon as the ambulance crew reported the nature of their findings.

Timms boarded the first bus that stopped and got off two stops later. He found a phone booth and dialled the number that he had received earlier in the week.

"I need to speak to the Commander, urgently", he said as soon as the line was connected.

"One hour."

Shortly before the hour was up Timms phoned the casualty department of the hospital. He tried to hide his Belfast accent as much as possible as he sought to convince the receptionist that he was a reporter from the Daily Record. I've just heard that some guy's been admitted leaking like a sieve from knife wounds. Is it going to be 'a murder in the West End' story or not?''

The silence at the other end was subjected to cajoling pleas before it finally broke.

"I don't think so. The patient has lost a lot of blood and we've counted fourteen separate stab wounds, but fortunately none of the vital organs have been damaged."

"So when do you think he can have visitors?"

"Couple of days, I expect. Doctor will know better. What do you want to know that for? I thought you said you were a reporter."

Timms cut her off and dialled the Belfast number again. He explained to McLean what he had found and what had been said.

"You're absolutely sure he said 'Sullivan'."

"There's not a lot of names that you could get mixed up with that one."

The Commander thought that sometimes Timms forgot about the hierarchical structure in the organisation and his remarks verged on insubordination. On this occasion he confused that with the anger in Timm's voice. Dillon had briefly mentioned to Timms that the Commander had allowed Peter to return unharmed and about the flight from the hotel before he could be collected. He had decided, however, to postpone both discussing the merits of this decision and informing his flat mate about his forthcoming crossing of the Atlantic until after they had eaten.

"Maybe I got that one wrong", said McLean softly.

Timms could not control his ire.

"Bloody right, you got it wrong. You should have at the bloody least let me know when he fucked off out of the "Dunaddry". Didn't that give you a clue that he might be thinking about doing something. And then you let John come back here without arranging protection."

"Calm down, Marshall. John wasn't supposed to come back to Glasgow. It was all arranged that he would go straight to another posting but he insisted on returning briefly just to pack. I think he wanted to say cheerio to you personally as well."

"Don't try to shift your guilt to me McLean, that won't work. What are we going to do about it now?"

"Exactly what I said we would do. Sullivan has to be executed. Will you do it or will I send somebody across?"

"No, this one's mine. John was a good friend. I'll enjoy it."

"OK. but don't screw it up and do it tonight. The closer the punishment is to the deed, the greater the deterrent value. Take one of the local boys along as a driver. When you've finished come back over here. I suspect that city will be like a cauldron for a while after people cotton on to what's happened. It'll be a small compensation to you Marshall, but I'd be surprised if I'm still your controller after this cock up. Thank fuck John's still alive."

Now Timms used the time waiting at the phone box to make a reservation with Manx airlines. When Egan arrived they drove straight to the "Derry Bar". The car stopped right outside its door and Timms entered with purpose and determination. He said simply to the first barman that came to attend to him.

"Peter Sullivan?"

"Not me, pal. That's the boss. The guy over there with the suit."

The barman indicated with a nod of his head, the figure sitting on a high stool behind the bar. Timms had almost reached the part of the bar closest to his intended victim as Peter picked up another bundle of the invoices and till receipts that he had been meticulously checking. He had found that attending to the business of the bar, provided for him a cathartic therapy. He had recalled his ordeal but also noted to himself that he had passed out of the other end of the darkness. It gave him strong hope that he would recuperate. Then he would set about to build an even better world for himself: just as his father had taken steps to carve out a new future. He would wear the albatross of the collections until he could work out a method of freeing himself. If this involved revenge on Dillon or his successor then that would be a bonus. Isabel would be replaced in this new world, probably not by Ann, but why shouldn't he, a successful businessman, have the pick of the many attractive women that were available in the city. He was awoken rudely from these thoughts.

"Sullivan." Timms barked.

Peter dropped the papers at the recognition of the accent. "Are you Timms?"

"Fucking right I am and this is for John, you papist bastard."

The pistol and Peter's hands were raised simultaneously. The bang caused the whole pub to be frozen in a moment in time. No one moved or spoke as they watched the landlord drop to the floor. By standing on the brass rail that ran around the bottom of the bar, Timms could see where Peter had fallen. The body was writhing in convulsive spasms.

Timms briefly recalled the evenings that he had sat in the council house in Portadown, its exterior decorated with Unionist flags and red, white and blue bunting. He and other young men had discussed the act and the art of assassination. All agreed that when undertaken in a public place it had to be completed with a single shot. The surprise element would have the effect of momentarily stunning any onlookers. Should the assailant, however, require to discharge a second or subsequent shot then they placed themselves at risk of being tackled by those whose sense of caution had not fully developed. 'Have a go merchants' they had called this breed. The recent image of Dillon's suffering quickly provided a powerful counter argument. Two more bullets were pumped into the body and it was stilled.

Timms left as purposefully and as calmly as he entered. The door of the car was open and as he got in it screeched away in second gear.

Sean seemed to be the first to drop from the state of suspended animation that enveloped the whole bar. His shout released the rest from their paralysis. There was a collective realisation that this moment signalled an end to the halcyon days that many had enjoyed in the "Derry Bar". Most of the customers and even a few of the staff decided to leave before the police arrived. They knew that they probably would not again cross the portals still blackened where the petrol had landed at the beginning of the story in which many of them had been unconscious participants.

"What was that all about?" said Egan "I heard three shots. You ran the risk of one of the punters tackling you."

"It was worth it for John. Drop me off at the next block."

Timms jumped out and after checking that he was not being observed placed the gun in a rubbish bin. He heard his driver shout through the open side window as he passed, "Best of luck, big man!"

He then walked a half mile through streets with which he was relatively familiar, crossed through Queen's Park and hailed a taxi to take him to the airport. Five minutes after losing his passenger, Egan was stopped in a police road-block. A constable approached the car to enquire from where he had come. This enabled him to note both that Egan was alone and spoke with a broad local accent and the car was allowed to proceed. As he returned to his duties in the road block, the young constable contemplated on the coincidence that both incidents he had attended that day involved the Irish community in the city. The previous one concerned a stabbing in the West End two hours or so earlier that day and he had assisted in searching the surrounding streets in the hope that he might come across a blood stained assailant.

He was aware that the detectives investigating that incident had learned from the neighbours that the two Irishmen who occupied the flat had lived there together for a number of years, that they rarely socialised but they were believed to frequent the ''Vintner's Bar'' on a regular basis. The last piece of information merely confirmed for Detective Inspector Mullen, the officer in charge of the case, that his initial assumption about the sexual proclivity of two men living together had been correct. One of the Irishmen was the victim, the other had been seen leaving the flat shortly before the ambulance had arrived and then had since failed to return or to make contact with the police.

The collective wisdom amongst the constable's colleagues that it was an open and shut case. The two Irishmen were obviously homosexual lovers who had had a tiff, perhaps related to the victim's recent time away from the flat that resulted in this outbreak of domestic violence. 'Un crime passionnel', the young constable had contributed to the debate. His older, more jaded and blasé colleagues glanced at him with a weary incomprehension and one of them whispered to himself, "Fucking Paddy poofters".

The headquarters of the Glasgow police force in St. Andrew's Square was an old Victorian building ill suited for modern police work. The hope amongst senior officers was that when the impending reorganisation of local government took place, new offices would be found to direct and manage the far larger force that would be formed. Until then D.I. Mullen had to share a cramped office with his colleague D.I. Campbell. The desks of these two faced each other and they were in the habit of freely commenting upon each other's cases.

Both Detective Inspectors were working late that evening. Mullen was completing a report on Dillon's stabbing and Campbell was awaiting the return of Detective Sergeant Fraser who had been assigned the task of informing Peter's widow of the incident in the "Derry Bar". Fraser had originally objected to this assignment suggesting that uniformed police officers would better prepare Mrs Sullivan for the shock, but his boss had insisted that it was undertaken by C.I.D officers.

"It's just possible that the widow will have

some vital information to impart. And if acted upon quickly it might just prevent the perpetrator from making good his escape from justice. The collection of that information is a C.I.D. function.''

Fraser was certain that Campbell used this Dickensian form of language that was banished now even in the type of formal reports that were sent to the procurator fiscal, only in his presence. It had the unsettling effect of making it more difficult for him to put across his arguments or suggestions as to how they should conduct enquiries.

When Fraser came into the office both D.I.s stopped the discussion between themselves and waited on his report.

''Didn't get to see Mrs. Sullivan, sir. But had a chat with the neighbours, a Mr and Mrs Anderson. Older couple live next door. Fill their lives by knowing everything in the street. Had some interesting things to tell us.''

When Fraser was in a recalcitrant mood he would take pains to use a staccato form of language that was diametrically opposed to the flamboyant loquaciousness employed by his superior. Campbell found it at best irritating and had told him not to speak in newspaper headlines. Fraser retorted that he was only trying to be pragmatically succinct.

''Pray, enlighten us as to the nature of these revelations.''

''Seems like the Sullivans' marriage was not

completely full of sweetness and light. Apparently they had a major blowout around about eleven o'clock this morning. Slapping each other about. But here's the interesting bit. The neighbours heard him accuse her of trying to have him killed and she replied that she would be doing so again, and this time they wouldn't fail."

Mullen leaned over his desk to interrupt, "Who is the 'they'."

"There, indeed, is the question. Does it sound to you as though she hired a professional hit man to do it?", enquired Campbell.

Fraser was unsure whether this question had been directed at him or the other D.I. He felt though that since he had had the direct contact with the reporters to this exchange, his response would be the more valuable.

"Yes sir, that occurred to me but I don't think it's a runner. Perhaps a bit dramatic. This isn't Dodge city or even Belfast. I don't think that you can go shopping and pick up a gunslinger's services just like that. The other more likely scenario is that she was having an affair and her lover did the dirty for her."

"You said though that Sullivan had already accused her of trying to have him killed." Mullen emphasised the phrase 'to have him killed' and continued, "that might indicate that she already had hired a killer and just made contact with him again."

Campbell could not hide his delight at the fact that Mullen had shot a gaping hole into his young officer's logic. He had felt that Fraser's dismissal of his theory had in fact been a challenge to his authority and, done in front of another officer, tantamount to usurping his position. He picked up his colleague's contention and continued the attack with relish.

"Just imagine, if you will, this situation. The killer has an attempt to do Sullivan in but bungles it in some way. Mrs Sullivan tells him that she will not pay for a botched job. He would then wish to complete the task as quickly as possible for he wants the reward and to postpone the undertaking would place him in jeopardy, particularly now that Sullivan would know that his life is in danger. This would explain why he has the audacity to carry out the task in a crowded bar and the three shots are explained by his frustration at failing the first time around."

He looked around his office with a smile of satisfaction.

"Don't worry Fraser. Experience gives you a feel for these things. Now get on with trying to find Mrs Sullivan and see if any of our informers have heard anything about a professional hit man arriving in the city in the last fortnight or so. Aye and while you're at it, sergeant, stick a couple of men at the Dublin and Belfast gates at the airport with a brief of the best description we've got of the character in the pub. And send it down to Stranraer as well, just in case."

Fraser deliberately let his superior complete his directions before he responded. "All done an hour ago, sir."

"Smart arse bastard," came the whispered, grudging praise.

After the sergeant had gone, Mullen rose to put on his coat and said, "I've done enough for one day. I'm going home. I'll finish this report in the morning."

Then, almost as an afterthought, he asked his colleague, "These two crimes both done by people with Irish accents. Descriptions not a hundred miles apart. Do you think there could be any connection?"

"Shouldn't have thought so. The man you are looking for is a homosexual so that means he is unlikely to be Mrs Sullivan's lover. I also think it makes it pretty unlikely that he would be a professional killer, otherwise he would have shot his lover if he wanted to harm him. Anyway the idea of a pansy being a hit man doesn't really fit in with the psychological profile, does it?"

Mullen reflected for a moment before replying, "Psychological profile. No I suppose it doesn't. Thank goodness I'm due for retirement before all these changes come in."

Chapter 21

The taxi soon found the motorway and headed west towards the airport. Timms reclined in the seat and buried himself deep in comforting thoughts. He used to fly frequently into this airport with his father who conducted his business, not only in Northern Ireland but in Scotland as well. In those days the airport location was always referred to as Abbotsinch after the small island in the River Cart that had once been the property of a religious order. Now it was simply known as Glasgow airport, but there was still no direct public transport system from the city centre. He mused that this fact perhaps should question the airport's right to use that new title but moved on to consider his forthcoming journey. He looked at his watch. Nine o'clock. It was dark now, but if all proceeded to schedule, he would be in the air in a Manx Airlines plane in a little under an hour. The lateness of the hour when he arrived at Douglas would necessitate him finding accommodation for the evening. That would be unlikely to cause major problems. The Isle of Man is a major holiday resort and now the high season had finished there would be a plethora of empty rooms to let even to a weary traveller passing through late at night. He would take an early morning ferry to Dun Laoghaire, taxi to Connolly Street Station and then catch the Dublin to Belfast express train. With a bit of luck in his connections he would be in Belfast mid afternoon the following day.

He wondered what the taxi driver would say if he told him of the plans for this circuitous journey. It was unlikely that the police would have covered the airport already but he saw no reason to run unnecessary risks. The Irish accent heard at the pub might have led them to put a surveillance team at the gates to the Dublin and Belfast flights.

He might have had a completely different set of thoughts had he known that Isobel had driven down this same road less than ten minutes earlier. She had started out by again following the pattern of taking random bends and turns, but then had decided that she had to leave the city to escape. She drove out along the M8 with a vague notion that she would deposit the car and get a flight to some exotic climes. Then it occurred to her that's precisely where the Police would be lying in wait for her. She drove past the airport saw the sign for Greenock and determined that that destination held nothing for her. The Erskine bridge allowed her to regain the north side of the Clyde. She drove for another two hours and then, totally exhausted, she looked for somewhere to stop. The lights of a pub on the other side of the road seemed to come on in answer to this prayer.

Angus was standing in the doorway in the process of ushering the evening's revellers out of "The Tight Line" when he was approached by the woman with the staring eyes and excited speech.

"Can you help me please. I need somewhere to stay tonight. Somewhere near here. I can't drive anymore."

"Do ye no see the lights of the hotel just where your motor car is parked."

Isobel turned and there was a large sign unlit but visible in the moonlight proclaiming the Loch Awe Hotel. Angus then saw that her hands and coat were stained blood red. She could feel him looking and in the light from the pub window learned of the reason for his curiosity.

"I stopped at a car accident on the Loch Lomond road. I must have picked this up then. And that's why I'm so late tonight. Do you think they will still have a room for me?"

"Now it would be a terrible injustice if after you having put yourself out for others we couldn't do the same for you. The hotel and the pub are owned by the same people. Come away in and I'll use this internal phone gadget to ask them to open the door to you."

From inside she could see through the window the lights at the front of the hotel come on in response to Angus's call. The night porter then came across and escorted her in to the grand mahogany panelled entrance hall of the hotel. An older lady who turned out to be the resident receptionist arrived shortly afterwards in her dressing gown and when Isabel started to apologise she brushed her protestations aside.

"Dinnae fash yerself, lassie. It's not any bother at all. We'll soon have you tucked up in a nice cosy bed. Do you want something to eat?"

Isabel found the kindness quite overwhelming and smiled a very grateful smile.

"No nothing thanks. I just want to get to bed."

"Of course you do. Owen will get the luggage and show you up to the room."

"Its all right. I haven't got any luggage with me. I didn't expect to be travelling overnight."

"No of course you wouldn't have. Is it a doctor or a nurse that you are?"

The quizzical look on Isabel's face was half hidden in the dim light of the hall.

"I'm sorry, I mean, I beg your pardon."

The old lady's face betrayed embarrassment as she explained, "Angus, the barman told us that the reason you had been delayed in your journey was that you had been helping at a motor car accident."

"Oh, yes of course. I'm a nurse. I just couldn't work out how you knew that."

Isabel followed the porter up the stairs to the bedrooms.

It was one of those old fashioned hotels with landings of shiny oak floors that matched the doors of the bedrooms. Owen had turned the brass handle and the door creaked open. He switched on the light and Isabel saw a large inviting bed in front of her. As soon as she was left alone, she threw herself on top of the bed and sought respite from her anguish through sleep. This mercy was to be denied her. She turned her body one way and then another seeking soporific sanctuary but her mind continued to operate at a level of full consciousness. Time and time again she saw herself going up the stairs of that common close in the West End of Glasgow. The drama that had been that day's events was played out again and again in her racing mind at a frenetic pace. The last scene consisted of her lover lying draped in a cloak of blood on the floor with her standing over him, still holding that terrible knife. The baying and screams for revenge from the audience were in effect her own feelings of guilt. She closed her eyes and tried to shut out these sounds but they merely grew louder. She prayed into herself to be allowed to sleep just on top of the bed and only for a few hours. In the morning she would have regained her composure and she would be able to work out what she must do. But still that torment of being involuntarily awake when the rest of the world is asleep persisted. Each sound outside was magnified by her heightened awareness. Rain started to gently tap on the window. It felt as though she was being summoned to observe the embryonic storm that was brewing over the dark waters of the loch.

She pulled back the curtains and watched in

silence for the few minutes that it took the rain to progress from a gentle shower to a torrential downpour. She spoke out loud and waited to hear whether her words would return to her in an echo.

"What a wild night."

The voice that responded however was not hers. "Sometimes the weather of the day reflects the passion of the soul."

She recognised the tones as being familiar to her. They were redolent of a time in her life when she felt protected and cherished but had difficulty in locating them in the bank of her memory. She knew that she should not be hearing them but felt neither fear nor doubt as she turned around.

Father Sorley was sitting on the ruffled bed smiling at her. Tranquility pervaded the ambience of the room and the priest spoke again.

"You're in a terrible state, lassie. Guilt is an awful thing."

She found herself kneeling beside him with her head placed on his lap. Her tears fell on to his black cassock and then she felt his hand gently stroke the back of her hair.

"What's to be done, Father. I killed a man today. I stabbed him in cold blood. Oh, you know I've never done anything like that before. I just wanted him to be there for me and for the baby. Tell me Father what have I to do now."

All this was said in a strangely peaceful voice;

the tones were hushed but not strained. The priest stood up and raised her by the shoulders until she was also standing facing him. He kissed her on both cheeks and helped her to sit again on the bed.

"You know what you should do, Isabel. You have always known and you knew as soon as you killed Dillon."

"I have to confess, don't I Father. Will you hear my confession?"

Father Sorley started to open the door to the lobby and then held it ajar.

"No, no Isabel. I can't do that. I only exist as part of you. I am that part of your past that remains as your conscience. For your confession to be effective it must be to someone that can give you that degree of absolution that you seek. You have to lay your soul bare before God, not before yourself."

She had found a towel and was busy wiping the tears away from her face. She conveyed her understanding with a smile. The priest raised his hand and directed a pointed finger towards her as he continued, "And you know that to find redemption on earth, you must also subject yourself to the laws of man. Without that first step you have little chance of redeeming your immortal soul. You do fully understand, don't you Isabel."

Before she had finished indicating her agreement to this last proposition, the priest left the room. She followed him into the lobby and with the assistance of the dim wall lights looked for him in both directions. She already knew though that he would not be in sight. She came back into the room and stripped naked. This time she climbed in between the sheets and slept a deep and peaceful sleep. When she came downstairs in the morning, she could see by the large black roman numbers in the face of the wall clock behind the reception desk that it was after ten o'clock.

It was a comforting 'good morning' that greeted her and she recognised the same receptionist as had assigned her a bedroom the previous evening.

"I'm afraid you're a wee bit late for breakfast. You must have been awful tired after all that driving and the accident and what not. But I'm sure we can get you some tea and toast if you would like that."

Isabel had to pause momentarily to realise to which accident she was referring, but accepted the offer of sustenance without hesitation. As she was writing out a cheque to pay her bill she enquired of the receptionist where she would be able to find a Catholic church.

"Well, there's one in Dalmally four miles south of here. Back on the Glasgow road. But if you don't want to retrace your journey the next one north will be in Oban."

"Would there be a Police Station in Dalmally?"

"Och no, it's just a wee place for such a thing. You would have to go to Oban for that as well."

Isabel thanked her profusely for all the kindness she had shown. She left the hotel, got into her car and headed up the shore of the loch towards Oban.

Chapter 22

The composure with which she walked from the hotel to the car park in front of the pub, indicated that a large weight had been lifted from her shoulder. Isabel smiled and said "Good Morning" to the few staff and guests that were still in the foyer. Outside, the storm had passed and the skies were clear. She could even feel a trace of the warmth of the sun stroke the side of her face. It was at one time sensual and reassuring.

From the recesses of her memory, the links with her past floated forth. She saw again Father Sorley's face, not in that hotel bedroom, but now in the school assembly hall. She could hear, deep within the same mind that only a few hours earlier had been her very own torture chamber, a cacophony of familiar and comforting sounds. As they became more and more distinct, she recognised them as the voices of her friends and classmates standing in front of Father Sorley, reciting answers from their Prayer Book. One of the questions given by the priest to the assembly dealt with the meaning of the word 'sacrament'. The answer that they had required to supply involved describing it as "an outward and visible sign of an inward and spiritual grace". The visitation in those early hours of this new day had been akin to receiving a sacrament. Now as she looked up at the purple clad hills that shelter the hotel she was removed from those events of the last twenty four hours. Peter, Dillon and the "Derry Bar" were ethereal. They existed only in her mind and their relevance to her future life would only be through her invitation. She also remembered that her future life was being carried within her womb. This child surely was the proof of her election. Then the coldness of reality chilled her.

When she went into her coat pocket to retrieve her car keys, she could not fail to notice the blood stains that still covered her coat. She took a handkerchief from her pocket and tried to wipe them away, but they had dried and fixed hard. The futility of her effort very quickly became so painfully obvious to her and she started to cry. Just as Lady MacBeth's hands would not wash clean nor would the smell of blood be removed by all the perfumes of Arabia, so too now did Isabel's stained coat become the omnipresent symbol of her deed.

The insubstantial and deceptive nature of her state of grace became apparent. She recalled the exhortation to confess to others. Sometimes Peter had cruelly teased Toto by letting him smell food but then placing it well out of his reach. Isabel harangued him to stop but she knew that it continued, usually when he returned late from one of his after hours drinking sessions. Only latterly had she realised that the cruelty arose from a displaced anger and in his mind it was she who was the victim of his power.

Now there was no such vicariousness, the teasing was directly targeted at her. She was being allowed to see Freedom in all its beauty and grandeur, just as it would surely soon be denied to her. She wondered what prison would be like. Her baby would be born there and would learn that the woman who gave it birth was the murderer of its father. The forgiveness through confession and repentance was not the property of God alone. The notion on which all her early faith had been based was a mirage. It looked real from a distance but as she had travelled the road that should lead to it, she had reached that critical point where it evaporates into the desert air. Father Sorley, she now understood, had come not with a promise of forgiveness but with a comfort that would allow her to gather the strength to face her punishment.

The scenery seemed to be more breathtaking around every bend that she drove. The peak of Ben Cruachan was shrouded in cloud, but as she continued through the pass it became more visible. She reached the village of Taynuilt and stopped. The top of the mountain was now completely clear and the sun seemed to shine down on it from only a few feet above it. She determined that she would return to this very spot when she was released from her jail sentence. She would resume her life then as though the two occasions had merged into one moment in time. That would be her reality and nothing would shake it.

The drive into Oban was now made with a sense of purpose. It was the start of a process through which she must pass. To enter into it was to demonstrate to herself that she again had control of her own destiny.

The young constable at the desk found the dirty shoddy look incongruous with the air of self confidence exuded by the woman standing in front of him. He was to be rocked again.

"My name's Isabel Sullivan of 27 Mearns Crescent, Glasgow. I want to tell you of a murder."

"A murder, Madam? Are you sure? We have no reports of any unaccounted bodies being found recently."

"This murder was committed yesterday in Glasgow."

It was obvious that the young policeman was having difficulty in determining whether he was the victim of a hoax or whether the woman was deranged or genuine. His tongue ran over his lips to compensate for the sudden dryness that he felt there. He knew that he would have to ask some more questions before he could seek the assistance of Sergeant McCuirtain.

"And were you in Glasgow at the time of the murder?"

"Yes."

"And why then did you not report this murder to the police in Glasgow?"

For some strange reason Isabel was reminded of the conversation with Dillon in the "Vintners" when she had first suggested that they have sex. She wondered whether this trait of being unable to accept that which is given too easily was in fact common to all males.

"I couldn't. I needed to get away. It was all a mistake. I never meant to kill him. He was going to leave me, you see and I'm carrying his baby, the poor little bastard."

Through the mist of incoherence an understanding formed.

"Are you saying Madam, that you committed this murder yesterday in Glasgow."

She had no idea that the actual act of admission would have been difficult. She looked at the policeman and saw the face of a young innocent boy. How could he possibly understand the love she felt for a terrorist, the loathing that she kept for her husband and the confusion of a tortured mind.

"Yes. I killed him. The police in Glasgow will know all about it by now. Perhaps you want to phone them."

The irritation was noticeable. "I'm sure that we shall follow the proper procedures, Mrs Sullivan. If you come through here the sergeant will be along in a minute to have a word with you."

The hinges creaked as a section of the long wooden desk was lifted up. Isabel was beckoned through the newly revealed entrance but she found herself involuntarily taking a step backwards.

"So you are arresting me?"

"Well we certainly want to speak to you a little more about this murder you're reporting."

She let her tense lips relax into a smile but before it had faded away she had fainted. She moved into a state of semi-consciousness a few minutes later but her incoherent ramblings were to cause all those in the station some considerable consternation.

An hour or so later in Glasgow, Detective Constable Fraser was returning from his morning tea break. He enjoyed all of these escapes from Campbell's sarcastic attentions and was in the process of calculating how long that it would be until lunch provided the next respite.

He entered the office that Campbell shared without any great relish for the tasks that he expected to be assigned, just at the moment the phone rang. The same level of enthusiasm was evident when his superior officer lifted the instrument. The change in his expression, however, was dramatic as Campbell became aware of the reason for the call. Both Fraser and Mullen stopped to watch a grin transform the usually sullen countenance. There was almost a ripple of a laugh in his tone as he responded to the dismembered voice at the other end of the line.

"Bloody right we are interested. I'm investigating that one. Put them through, will you?"

His observers realised that the call must indicate a significant development in one of the cases that were represented by the pile of buff folders strewn over the desk in front of him. Campbell's hand was moved to cover the mouthpiece. He ushered them closer to share the esoteric news.

"That murder, yesterday. It's the switchboard to say that Oban Police Station is asking whether we are interested in interviewing a Mrs Peter Sullivan. Seems she wants to tell us everything."

A few seconds later the dull tone was replaced by a distinct West Highland accent. "Hello, Detective Inspector. It's Sergeant McCuirtain here. I understand that it is yourself that wishes to speak to an Isabel Sullivan about a serious incident that occurred in Glasgow yesterday."

"No Sergeant, I want to speak to Mrs. Sullivan about a murder."

"Aye, that's what she said herself. She seems such a nice lassie. You can never really tell, can you now?"

Campbell peremptorily dismissed this last question as totally irrelevant and continued in a tone that he hoped would convey to his colleague that the gravity of the issue precluded such digressions.

"I need to know where the woman is now, Sergeant. I presume you are holding her."

"I'm afraid that she fainted at the front desk. Then, as she came to, she started to mumble something about her penance for the terrible deed she committed and finding peace. Then she kept on talking about being surrounded by priests who were trying to wrestle the knife out of her hands. We were worried about her and so we sent her up to the hospital. It seems that she is pregnant as well.''

Campbell's face was visibly turning redder and redder as he listened. He barked his next question. ''Is she alone?''

McCuirtain hid his anger over the implication of his incompetency. ''No sir. There's a WPC with her but she's just called in to say that the Doctor has requested a Mental Health Officer. It seems that he believes she should be sectioned under the terms of the Mental Health Act. He says that she is suffering from paranoid schizophrenia''

''Schizophrenic. Well, maybe you need some sort of a split personality to kill the person you live with.''

The recent discussion with the doctor had been relayed to the sergeant in some detail and he took pleasure in regaling Campbell with his new found knowledge.

''It would seem that delusions and hallucinations are classic symptoms of the disorder.''

''I'm sorry to hear all of this because it's important that we talk to Mrs Sullivan as soon as possible. We've got to find out who the character was that she hired to kill her husband.''

The momentary silence should have given advance notice of the confusion. When he did speak, the sergeant's voice was apologetic in tone.

"I'm sorry sir. There seems to be a bit of a mix up. Mrs Sullivan definitely told the WPC on the way to the hospital that it was her boyfriend that she had killed. She wanted to leave her husband for him and she certainly gave us the impression that she had stabbed him, herself. It would appear that he is a Protestant, she's a Catholic and that is preventing them from getting together. It's a wee bit hard for us up here to understand but I know that madness exists in Glasgow. You shouldn't send your kids to different schools."

Campbell usually reacted vehemently to pontifications from lower ranking officers, but on this occasion simply thanked the sergeant for his advice and advised him that he would be in Oban in a couple of hours to see Mrs Sullivan for himself. When he put the phone down, he rested his head in his hands.

"I think we might be able to close that case of the Irishman being stabbed yesterday."

Mullen in particular looked puzzled, "What do you mean? It was the Sullivan case that they were phoning up about wasn't it? And what was that business about split personalities and schizophrenia?"

The last question of the barrage was the one that burned like a beacon at the front of Campbell's consciousness. It symbolised for him the recognition of such familiar territory.

"It's this city that's fucking schizophrenic", he answered.

Cover Design

The cover design is by Anita Garnham, Design Associate Criffel Books. It highlights some important elements that feature within "Cuckoo Plot". The cross is representative of both the dagger that stabbed Dillon and of the Crucifixion. As such it symbolises at once the guilt felt by Isabel during the unfurling of the story and the guilt she has carried with her for all of her life. It hangs at an angle over the landscape redolent of the slant that Dali used in his famous painting. Under this Isabel and Dillon first discuss the impact of religious indoctrination on their younger minds - neither aware of the forthcoming dramatic impact of guilt and the search for redemption.

The cross cuts through the chain link fence. A fence that both binds and separates not just individuals but whole communities. Within the links are to be found the two colour sets of the sectarian divide that provides the backcloth to this story.

Beneath this fence are the tenement buildings of a Glasgow landscape. Both sides of the street converge on a site of urban wasteland, derelict, save for a single building. Its light is both a welcome for the Irish emigrés to the city and the passion that emanated from Sullivan's survival strategy.

Finally within the cross, the two words of the title form another cross. This is the double cross that is the "Cuckoo Plot".